ROBBY BRAVEHEART

ROBBY BRAVEHEART

DAVID KREWSON

Tate Publishing & Enterprises

Published by Tate Publishing & Enterprises, LLC
127 E. Trade Center Terrace | Mustang, Oklahoma 73064 USA
1.888.361.9473 | www.tatepublishing.com

Tate Publishing is committed to excellence in the publishing industry. The company reflects the philosophy established by the founders, based on Psalm 68:11,
"The Lord gave the word and great was the company of those who published it."

Book design copyright © 2010 by Tate Publishing, LLC. All rights reserved.
Cover design by Kristen Verser
Interior design by Blake Brasor

Published in the United States of America
ISBN: 978-1-61739-122-4
1. Fiction, Coming Of Age
2. Fiction, Christian, General
10.09.20

Robby Wilson stood in the dimly lit narthex, contemplating the odd-looking object on the small table. A clear plastic tube stuck in a six-inch square wooden base. It was placed beside what he had figured out to be a model of Noah's ark. The tube was about three feet high and was filled with quarters to about two-thirds of its height. It had been emptied just before Christmas and was filling up faster than usual. He shivered uncontrollably from being cold, wet, and scared. Could he go through with it?

Robby had noticed the tube the spring before when he occasionally came to the Wednesday after-school program at the church with some of his friends. The only other times Robby could remember being in a church were the few times they visited his dad's parents in Illinois when he was a small child. His parents would never go, and that didn't sit well with Grandma and Grandpa. Robby had always felt out of place and couldn't make sense out of what they were talking about.

Now he was a freshman in high school and was too old for the after-school program, but he came almost every week to walk his sixth-grade sister home. None of her friends lived near their home, and his mother thought it was too far for Cassie to walk home alone. His dad thought she didn't need to go at all.

Robby had watched the quarter tube fill up as the weeks went by, and then suddenly it would be empty and would start to fill up with quarters from the bottom again. He wondered how much money was in the tube when it was full to the top. *Two hundred dollars, I'll bet*, he thought to himself.

Late last spring the factory where Robby's dad had worked since he graduated from high school closed down, and the automobile parts they had made now came from another country. His dad had tried to find another job with other automotive plants in the area, but they were all cutting back on their workforce. Jack also looked for work in other industries and even checked out re-training programs that he heard about but found them to be flooded with other people in his situation. Frustrated and discouraged, he decided to just wait it out.

But now, eight months later, the job situation was much worse. Robby's mother had seen her full-time hours as a checkout clerk at Walmart cut to twenty-five hours. Sally Wilson was now supplementing those hours by working at Burger King and was working over fifty hours a week, sometimes going from job to job on the same day. About the only time Robby, Cassie, and seven-year-old Megan got to see their mother anymore was when she was going to work or getting home from work, usually out of sorts and too tired to have anything to do with them. Not at all what they had been used to.

When he wasn't out looking for work or doing odd jobs that he was able to pick up, Jack did most of the cleaning, shopping, cooking, laundry, and carting the children to all of their activities. But endless waiting in line to fill out job applications and never knowing when an odd job might pop up made it difficult for him to keep any kind of a schedule. That led to things like late dinners, his children having to find rides home from somewhere, or Sally getting home from work only to find out she had to go right back out and pick up a stranded child. Over time, Robby and his sisters noticed a strain between their parents that had not been there before. The money simply didn't stretch far enough, and they had no health insurance, which was all they talked to each other about anymore. When they talked at all.

In the fall, Robby had noticed that there always seemed to be some collection effort going on in the church. Clothing, new baby supplies, food, anything that poor people might need. He started taking things that his family needed, mostly food, usually cereal and canned vegetables. He would slip a can of vegetables in the back of the pantry almost every week, and so far his dad hadn't noticed. He would hide the cereal in his room and eat it there in order to stretch the family supply. There were many arguments with his dad about not eating breakfast, frequently ending with Robby storming off to school, slamming the door behind him.

The idea of taking the quarters began to grow in his mind after he leafed through one of the magazines lying on the table beside the ark. It was full of pictures and stories about people from other countries who didn't have enough food. Robby figured out that the quarters were probably being sent to those people. Then he started thinking that his family's situation wasn't that much different from the people in the magazine.

As time wore on, he started planning a way to empty the tube and get away without anyone seeing him. The only time he came to the church was around five o'clock on Wednesdays to pick up Cassie, and he couldn't do it with her around. If he came at another time people would wonder what he was doing there. No one from the church knew him, and on the few occasions that he encountered anyone in that area they always asked if they could help him. He would always mumble, "No thanks," and hurry back toward the gym to collect Cassie.

The area where the quarters sat was open to view on three sides—the main double-door entrance from the drop-off ramp on one end, two double doors opening out into the main church at the other end, and the church offices along one side. The secretary's office had a large window facing the narthex so she could see people coming in and out. The other side was the sanctuary, which had three entrances that were always closed.

One Wednesday Robby got to the church early and decided to do some exploring. He checked the tube and saw that the quarters were nearing the top. There was a door at one side of the sanctuary that led down a long hall and took him around to an area behind the sanctuary. It was cluttered with boxes, robes, musical instruments, and other things that meant nothing to him. *If I could grab the tube, get quickly to the door and into the hallway, I could take my time emptying the tube into my backpack,* he thought. Then the only problem would be getting back out into the narthex without being seen. He went back down the hallway and flipped the light switch as he went through the door. The light didn't go off. He turned around and saw that another light had gone on at the other end of the hall. Robby flipped the switch again, and the light at the far end went off.

Perplexed, he looked around for another switch when a gruff voice asked, "What are you doing?"

Frightened out of his wits, Robby turned to see a large, imposing man standing in front of him. He had seen the man around the church before and wondered if he worked there. "I can't … the light won't go off," Robby stammered.

"That light stays on all the time; there's no switch for it." The big man smiled, and his voice softened. "Are you here with the after-school kids?"

"No, I go to the high school. I'm just here to pick up my little sister. I was bored and was just looking around when I saw the light on." This man seemed really nice.

"Well, thanks for being responsible. I wish the members of this place would think about turning off the lights when they leave. I'm always shutting them off after somebody," he said as he headed toward the sanctuary doors.

Robby watched him go through the doors and then let out a sigh of relief. *That was close*, he thought. *What if I had been at the other end of the hall? How would I have explained that? With that light on all the time, it would be too dangerous to come back out that way. And I can't put the tube back. I'll have to hide it back in that room and find another way out.*

The next week Robby saw that the tube had been emptied and there were only a few quarters in the bottom. That, coupled with his close call the week before, convinced him to put his plan on hold. It was getting close to Christmas, and he noticed there was more activity in that area of the church. He stuck a couple of cans of vegetables in his backpack and decided to stay out of there until after the holidays. He didn't want to encounter anyone else who might remember him.

Christmas had been a disaster at their house. His mom had signed their family up to get food for the holidays from a food bank, and his dad had angrily made her remove their name from the list. "We don't need charity from anyone," he fumed. "I can provide for my family myself."

"Well, then why don't you?" Sally shot back and locked herself in the bathroom.

Robby knew she was in there crying and wished he could think of something to say to her. He didn't want to have another argument with his dad. He was thankful that his sisters weren't home to hear it. He had never seen his dad that angry.

Christmas morning was not fun for anyone. They had always had an artificial tree, but Jack wouldn't participate in decorating it. Robby had done the best he could putting it together. His mom complimented him for his efforts, but he knew it wasn't as good as his father would have done.

The girls woke up early but went into Robby's room until their parents got up. The presents under the tree were meager. Robby had saved his money from shoveling snow and walked his sisters to the dollar store to get something for their parents. They were able to get some body lotion for their mother and aftershave for their dad. The stockings were half filled with fruit and a small amount of candy. The children's gifts were limited to socks, underwear, and a two-dollar gift certificate to McDonald's. There was no exchange of gifts between Jack and Sally.

He couldn't just stand there looking at it; he had to do something. School had been snowed out, but the church had been open. He knew the secretary—Nancy, he had heard someone call her—left at four, so he slipped in the door when she wasn't looking and hid in the room behind the sanctuary. There was a door from that room into the sanctuary that would allow him to avoid the lighted hall when he made his escape. He had made sure that Nancy was gone and was out of excuses. He grabbed the tube, went through the door, and ran down the hall to the room behind the sanctuary. Out of breath and almost dizzy with fear, Robby upended the pipe and dumped the quarters into his already opened backpack. He stood there with the tube and base in his hand, frantically looking for a place to hide them. *Why didn't I figure that out while I was waiting?* he thought. He spied a cupboard standing just away from the wall. He pulled it out a little farther, stuffed the tube and base behind it, and then shoved it back to the wall as far as he could. Then he zipped up his backpack and went out into the sanctuary.

It was nearly dark outside, but the light that filtered through the stained-glass windows seemed like broad daylight to Robby. He felt totally exposed in the cavernous sanctuary and was thoroughly frightened. Sweating in spite of the coolness of the room, he walked quickly up the side aisle and paused at the door. *What if someone is on the other side like before?* he worried. He peeked through the small windows but didn't see anyone. Taking a deep breath, he pushed through the doors, hurried through the narthex out into the common area, and headed toward the back of the church.

Robby passed through the door to the classroom and preschool wing and was startled by the singsong alarm that went off whenever the door was opened. Those alarms had been installed to monitor the movements of any preschoolers who might decide to stray off. He moved down the long hall and pushed open the door into the vestibule, which also had an alarm. He had his hand on the door to the parking lot when headlights flashed past and a car pulled up along the curb right in front of the door. Robby watched the big custodian emerge from the car.

Panicked, he quickly backed out of the vestibule into the hall. He couldn't run down the hall; the man would be inside before he could get around the corner. He was next to a recessed entranceway that led into a classroom. The door was locked; he was out of time.

Paralyzed with fear, Robby cowered down in the back corner of the recess nearest the vestibule door. He heard voices and the key being turned in the locked exterior door. It wasn't voices; it was *a* voice. The custodian was talking on his cell phone. The alarm ding-donged as the man came into the hall. Robby watched him go past, the cell phone pressed to his ear blocking his view of the recess.

Robby sat there trembling, listening to the fading footsteps. "I still can't go out," he moaned to himself. *He'll hear the alarm.* Then he heard the alarm at the other end of the hall. Robby realized that the man had gone into the other part of the church and probably wouldn't hear the alarm on this door. *Even if he does hear it, he'd never get back here in time to see me,* Robby decided. He got up, pushed through both doors, and went out into the darkness. He ran around the back of the church and headed toward the safety of the street.

CHAPTER 2

It had dropped below freezing, but Robby was shivering more from being scared than he was being cold. He headed down a side street away from the church, toward his house, wondering if he would have to explain where he had been. His dad seemed to question everything he did. He had started out the day shoveling their drive and sidewalks and then went around knocking on doors to do it for money. He worked until three o'clock, except for treating himself to lunch at McDonald's, and then headed to the church, worried that he wouldn't get inside before Nancy left and locked the doors. He was frozen to the bone, and his feet were wet. He had hoped to warm up in the church, but the room he hid out in seemed as cold as outside.

He rounded the corner and saw his mother's car in the driveway but not his dad's truck. It was usually the other way around. His mother was sitting on the couch sipping a cup of tea and watching TV and didn't hear him come in. It was unusual to see his mother relaxing.

He stuffed his backpack under his bed, said hi to his sisters, who were playing in their room, and went back to the living room.

"Hi, Mom. Where's Dad?" he asked.

"Oh, hi, Robby. He's going to be late. So is supper," she answered with a smile in her voice.

"Why?"

"Someone he knows called him this morning to help him plow snow. Somebody called in sick, and with all this snow he needed help. Dad's bringing pizza."

"Are you home early?"

"No, you're home late. Where have you been all this time?" Sally asked.

"Shoveling snow," he said, handing her thirty dollars.

"Robby! You can't give us your money. You worked hard to earn it." Sally was near tears.

"You work hard to earn your money, and you do it all the time. I thought I could help."

"But you're just a child … but you're not, are you?" She got up and hugged him. "How could I not notice that?"

Robby didn't say anything. He just hugged her back.

"Robby," said his mother, stepping back and putting her hands on his shoulders. "We're going through a rough time, but it's not your responsibility. You do a lot to help around here, and your dad and I both appreciate it. It might not seem like we do sometimes, but we do. I would like you to keep this money for things that come up that you probably wouldn't ask us for money for. Like doing things with your friends—movies, McDonald's, whatever. I know you helped your sisters with Christmas. That would take some worry away from your dad and me, and you would decide how your money is spent, not us."

"Okay," he said, taking the money back. "I just don't like it that you have to work all the time. I want everyone to be happy."

"I'm so proud of you." His mother hugged him again—really hard this time.

Back in his room later that evening, Robby was nervously trying to count the quarters and put them in wrappers he had picked up from the bank. He would hear someone coming and quickly cover them up and pretend he was doing homework. Then he would have to start counting all over again. The only time someone actually came in was when his dad tapped at the door.

"Can I come in?" he asked.

"Sure."

Jack walked in and set down on the bed. "Mom told me about the money you offered to give us. That was pretty special. I don't think there are many kids your age who would do that. I couldn't be any prouder."

"Just trying to help," he said softly. Robby wanted to cry.

"But you do help. You keep the grass cut, the snow shoveled; you watch after your sisters. You're fourteen years old, Robby; you should be spending more time with your friends like you used to. That's why I agree with your mother about the money. Take it and use it to do stuff with your friends."

Robby lay on his bed for a long time after his dad left, thinking about all the things he had said to him. The evening meal had been like it was before his dad had lost his job—everybody laughing and joking, his sisters being silly like girls were supposed to. But that was just tonight. Dad wasn't going to plow snow tomorrow. He said he had been paid over a hundred dollars today. How long was that going to last? They needed a hundred dollars every day.

He had given up counting the quarters for the night and shoved them and the wrappers under his bed. He had only managed to count out two rolls, and it looked like there were still a lot left. He hoped so.

Now what was he going to do with the quarter money? He thought he was going to be helping with expenses, like groceries or the house payment or gas for the cars. Now he was just going to spend it on himself. Robby was starting to have serious regrets about what he had done.

CHAPTER 3

Don hung up the phone, perplexed. Why would someone move the peace pipe? And where did they put it? A friend from church had called, asking why the peace pipe wasn't on the table. She had some quarters to put in on Sunday and didn't see it anywhere in the narthex. Don called the church office, but no one there had any idea where it was. He mentioned it to some others at Bible study that evening and got the same results. They were starting to think someone might have stolen it.

The next morning Don got a call from his friend Bob. "Hi, Don, I found your peace pipe."

"Where was it?"

"Back in the sacristy, wedged in behind a cupboard. I saw a corner of the base sticking out, so I moved the cupboard, and there it was—empty."

"Just like we suspected. What were you doing in the sacristy?"

"Looking for the peace pipe." Bob chuckled. "I decided to come over and look for it because it didn't think anyone would try to carry it out of the church."

"What made you think to look back there?" Don asked.

"Well, I just started thinking where I would hide the thing if I was going to steal the money."

"How could you think like that? You're a sick man."

"I found it, didn't I?" Bob laughed.

"We'll never find out who took it. Like we talked last night, I hope they really needed the money."

"Thankfully there was no after-school program last week, so the kids won't get blamed. It had to be someone who is familiar with the church. Just a casual visitor wouldn't even know there was a room back there," Bob reasoned.

"I still think I'm going to ask Jay if I can speak to the after-school kids on the off chance that they might know something," said Don. "Plus, it might just be a teaching moment we shouldn't pass up. I'll let Jay decide."

Robby managed to get the rest of the quarters counted and wrapped by the weekend. He was disappointed. He had expected almost twice as much. "I took someone else's money and risked getting caught for fifty-eight dollars and twenty-five cents," he muttered to himself. He felt good that his parents had confidence in him to spend the money wisely on himself and his sisters, but he was worried that they could lose their home or someone would get sick. And he couldn't shake the feeling of guilt. What would his parents think of him if they found out?

He was afraid they would ask questions at the bank if he traded all the quarters in at once, so he just took one roll in on Monday. The friendly teller asked him how long it had taken him to save up all those quarters. He mumbled something about a family project, took the ten dollars, and left. *I can't go to the bank every week with a roll of quarters,* he thought. Then someone would get suspicious. *Maybe I'll just take a roll in when I need some money.* He was planning to stretch the money out as far as possible.

Robby went to the church a little later than usual on Wednesday, nervous about being there at all, but he had to wait anyway. Cassie and a few other kids were in an animated conversation with the youth minister, Jay, who ran the after-school program, and an older man who seemed to be doing a lot of explaining. Robby waited by the door to the gym and couldn't hear what anyone was saying. He could tell the kids were very interested in what the man was saying.

They weren't even out the door when Cassie asked him, "Have you ever noticed that pipe thing in the front part of the church that people put quarters in?"

"Yeah."

"It's called a peace pipe."

"Okay."

"It's called Heifer Project. They're trying to solve world hunger. They think if people aren't hungry it will be easier to have peace."

Robby waited. "That's why they call it a peace pipe," Cassie said finally.

"I got that part."

"Don says they—"

"Who's Don?" Robby interrupted.

"He's that man we were talking to with Jay. He takes care of Heifer Project for the church. He told us they teach poor people all over the world how to take care of animals like cows and sheep and goats and pigs, and then they give them some pregnant ones to get milk and wool and stuff from, but they have to give the babies away so someone else can have animals." Robby wondered if she was ever going to stop to breathe. "It's called 'passing on the gift.' And they can't eat them," she added.

"So that's what happens to the quarters?" he asked.

"Yeah, people all around the country are putting their quarters in peace pipes. This church has sent more than five thousand dollars to Heifer."

Minus fifty-eight dollars and twenty-five cents, thought Robby. He wasn't feeling very good about himself.

"Somebody took it," said Cassie after a while.

"Took what?" asked Robby, already knowing.

"The peace pipe. They emptied it out and hid it in a room somewhere, but somebody found it. That's why Don came to talk to us."

"What did he say?" Robby was getting nervous.

"He said at first they were really upset, but after thinking and praying about it, they hoped that whoever took the quarters really needed the money to get through some hard times. That's what it was for in the first place."

"Do they think they know who took it?"

"Don't have a clue. But they're asking around to see if anyone knows who it is, so if they do need help, maybe the church can do something for them."

"They would help somebody who stole from them?" Robby didn't know what to think.

"That's what Don said."

That night at dinner, Cassie told the story all over again, adding some details that she hadn't told Robby earlier. "Don showed a video of a bunch of places all over the world where Heifer has projects that help poor people. Asia, Africa, South America, even in our country—a lot of them, Don said.

"There's a story about a girl in Africa named Beatrice whose family got a goat. Beatrice is nine, but she's never been to school because her family is too poor to buy a uniform or books. All she has to wear is a red dress, and it has a bunch of slits in it to make it bigger so she can get it on because it's too small for her. Their goat has twins, but they only have to give one away, so they are rich now because of selling goat milk.

At least, rich for where they live. So now she gets to go to school. She's really smart and caught up with kids her own age in only two years.

"They wrote a book about her, and some people saw it and gave her a scholarship to college here in the US. She wants to be a vet and go back to her village and take care of people's animals. Don and his wife got to meet her when she was sixteen, and she signed one of her books for them. He had it with him, and we got to look at it a little bit. I asked him if I could read it, and he let me bring it home. I have to take it back next week."

"Can I see it?" asked Megan.

"Sure, you can read it if you want."

"Maybe you could read it to me," said Sally.

"Okay." Megan smiled, seeing a chance to get some much-needed attention from her mother.

"I'll listen too," Cassie piped in, wanting to get in on the action. "I'd probably read it twice anyway."

Back in his room, Robby was having trouble concentrating on his homework. He and his dad had listened to the story as well. Everyone liked the story, especially because it was true. Robby couldn't get his mind off the photograph they found stuck in the book of the girl signing it for Don and his wife. *She was poorer than me, but she didn't steal anything,* he kept thinking. He had leafed through the book and noticed an address label stuck on the inside of the back cover. He looked the name up in the phone book and wrote down Don's number. *How can I give the money back without anyone knowing it?* he wondered.

And he couldn't put aside what Cassie said about the church helping whoever took the money. Was it a trick, or did they mean it?

CHAPTER 4

Cassie had made some good friends at the after-school program who talked her into going to Sunday school. She and her mom worked it out that Sally would drop Cassie off on her way to work, which was in the middle of the first church service. Cassie would then wait in the gathering area until her friends came out of church. After a few weeks, she started slipping into the back of the sanctuary to see the end of the service. Then one of her friend's mother said to her, "Cassie, you don't have to sit in the back of the church by yourself. Please come up and sit with us. We would like that." So she did.

When Cassie started going to church, Robby asked her if anyone ever said anything about the stolen money. "I never heard any more about it since Don talked to us that time," she told him.

Robby was becoming more and more troubled about taking the money. He hadn't spent any of it and had pretty much decided he wasn't going to. He wanted to give it back but couldn't think of a way to do it without the risk of getting caught. The thought of that terrified him. What would his parents think? What would his sisters think? What would anyone think? Everyone would know he was a thief. It wouldn't matter that he gave it back; no one would ever trust him again.

He couldn't understand why he kept thinking that he should talk to Don; why he thought he could help him. Robby had picked up the phone and started to dial Don's number several times but hung up because he had no idea what he would say to him. Don had said that the church would help someone who really needed it, even though they stole from them. Maybe that's why he thought he should talk to Don.

Robby knew that his parents were barely making ends meet. The tension had lessened and his parents were getting along better since the snowstorm. His dad had been asked to help again the next day, and that helped the money situation a little bit. From the beginning Jack seemed to find odd jobs every week or so, which kept them from getting farther behind. But it wasn't enough, and Robby still worried about it. *What if they take our house? What if one of us gets sick?* He picked up the phone.

"Hello," said Don.

"Is this Don?"

"It is."

"Are you there?" Don asked after a long silence.

"I'm calling for a friend."

"Okay, what can I do for your friend?"

Robby let out a big breath. "You know those quarters someone took?"

"Does this have something to do with your friend?"

"Yes."

"Your friend knows who took them?"

"My friend took them."

"And you're going to rat your friend out?" *How old is this kid? Middle school? High school?* Don wasn't sure.

"No! No, I want to help my friend," Robby exclaimed.

"Is your friend having regrets about taking the money?"

"Yes, my friend wants to give it back but is afraid of getting caught."

"I'm listening."

"Well, my friend's family is going through a really bad time. The dad lost his job last spring, and the mom is working two jobs. They don't have any health insurance, and they can barely make their house payments. My friend is afraid they could lose their house or one of them could get sick. So my friend thought that the money would help with expenses." It all just rushed out. It felt good to tell someone, even a stranger.

"Are you the only one your friend has told about this?" *Or are you calling for yourself and there is no friend?* Don almost added.

"Yes."

"Okay, you don't want to betray your friend, but your friend's family needs help. How can we help your friend's family if we don't know who they are?" asked Don.

"What about the money?"

"We can work that out later. We need to figure out how to help this family until the dad finds a job. When a young person is so worried about their family that they would steal to help them, we need to take that seriously. Between you and me, we can help your friend give the money back without anyone but us knowing it. But let's solve the big problem first."

"You're not mad?" Robby couldn't believe it.

"About what? At who?"

"At my friend for taking the money."

"Well, actually, I was at first. I thought it was a pretty lowlife thing to do. But after talking it over with a lot of my friends, we decided that it was probably someone who was desperate. At least we hoped that the money would help someone. Turned out to be true, didn't it?"

"Yeah, but it's not going to help if my friend gives it back," said Robby.

"No, but maybe this family will get some help that it would not have if your friend hadn't taken the money. Maybe the devil didn't make your friend do it; maybe God did."

"What?" said Robby. He had no idea what Don was talking about.

"Do you go to church?" Don asked.

"No."

"Does your family belong to a church?"

"No." Robby sighed. *What's he trying to find out?*

"Have you ever been to our church?"

"Just a few times to that after-school program last year," Robby lied. *I can't let him know I go there every week*, he thought.

"Why didn't you keep coming?"

"It was last spring, and I go to the high school now."

"Well, my young friend … do I get to know your name?"

"No."

"Okay. Well, my young friend, many of us believe that God sometimes causes things to happen in our lives whether we want him to or not."

"Did God make my friend's dad lose his job?" Robby asked just a little sarcastically.

"I doubt it." Don smiled to himself. *Did I strike a nerve?* he wondered. "God gave us the free will to do whatever we want but at the same time made it clear that we would pay the consequences for making bad choices. A lot of people have made a lot of bad choices for a long time, and now a lot of other people are suffering for it. Your friend's family is a good example of that. And also, your friend chose to take the money, which your friend knew was wrong, and is now paying the consequences of a guilty conscience. Which is why you called me. Right?"

"Right."

"So what do you think about God?" Don asked.

Robby paused, not sure what to say. "I don't think about it. I don't know anything about that stuff," Robby answered. He didn't like the way this was going.

"You don't wonder why things exist? How the world got made? What happens when we die?"

"Sometimes."

"How often is sometimes?"

"I do wonder about some of that stuff but not all the time," Robby confessed.

"Often enough to come to church and give us a chance to help you understand it?" Don asked.

Robby was starting to feel trapped. "All I wanted to do was find out how my friend could give the money back without getting in trouble." *Maybe I should just keep the money. This guy is going to find out who I am.* Robby thought about hanging up.

"Does your friend know you're calling me?"

"Yes."

"How did you get my name?"

"My friend got it from someone who heard you talk about Heifer at the after-school program."

That's interesting, thought Don. *Either he is not in high school and comes on Wednesdays, or he knows someone who does. There was no after-school program that week because of the snow, so it's still a mystery when he did it. I'd sure like to know. I have to flush this kid out into the open.*

"Okay, in order for your friend to return the money, one of you has to trust me. You don't know me. For all you know, I'm just trying to find out who you are so I can bust your friend. It's quite natural for you to think that, and I understand. My feelings aren't hurt. So you talk this over with your friend and come up with a plan to return the money. But what's more important is for our church to help this family. Find out everything you can about their needs. We can provide food, money to help with the mortgage or health care. You have my number; call me in a week."

CHAPTER 5

Don had just hung up the phone as his wife returned from her walk on the treadmill. Lucy had started down the stairs to the basement when the phone rang. She hesitated until she could tell it wasn't for her and then continued on her way.

"That was a long conversation," she said, plopping herself down in a chair across from him. "Who was it?"

Don contemplated his answer. "Well, I don't know his name, but I'm almost certain it's the person who took the quarters."

"Really? What did he say?"

"I promised him I wouldn't tell anyone, so we never had this conversation," said Don.

Lucy smiled. *How many times have we said that to each other over the last fifty years?* "Okay. I've forgotten most of it already," she promised.

"He claimed he was calling for a friend who had taken the quarters and is filled with remorse and wants to return them."

"You don't believe him."

"I wondered at first, but after a while it seemed unlikely. He knew too many details."

"Like what?" Lucy asked.

"Like all the problems his friend's family was having. Dad out of a job, mom working two, no health insurance. That's a lot of details for fourteen-year-old boys to share."

"He told you his age?"

"He said he had been to the after-school program last year but is now in high school."

"What else did he tell you?"

"He said that except for coming to our after-school program several times, he had only been in a church a few times in his entire life. His concept of God was like no concept at all. He said, in effect, the possibility of God rarely ever entered his mind," Don went on.

"You asked about that?"

"Yes."

"So how did you leave it?"

"Well, I really think it's important to find out if this family is in such trouble that a fourteen-year-old would feel the kind of desperation that I sensed. And if they are, we need to help them. You know we all talked about that when we were speculating about who might have taken the money and why. I hoped we would help them. I hope it wasn't just talk. I told him maybe God made him take the money to give us a chance to help his family. And I meant not just with money."

"Maybe you're right. So how did you leave it?" Lucy asked again.

Don smiled. "I told him he and his friend needed to trust me in order to make it work. I said they needed to come up with a way to return the money and then call me again. I said call me in a week."

"Let's pray that he does."

Robby put the phone back in the cradle. He was angry, confused, still very uneasy that he was going to be exposed, and strangely hopeful that things were going to be all right. Angry because Don thought he was calling to snitch on a friend. Confused that Don seemed more concerned about helping his family than he was getting the money back. Uneasy because he got the feeling Don knew he wasn't calling for a friend.

The hopeful thing was a real mystery to him. He couldn't remember the last time he felt hopeful. It seemed as though all he did was worry. Why would a whole bunch of people want to help someone who had stolen from them? Robby just couldn't understand it, nor could he stop thinking about it. *Don made it sound like they were already talking about what they could do to help, and they don't even know we exist.*

The toughest thing right now was that Don expected him to figure out how to return the money. "Talk it over with your friend and come up with a plan," he had said. Robby had expected Don to figure that out. *And I don't have a friend I can talk to about it. All I do is talk to myself. Argue with myself. And why did he ask me about God?*

CHAPTER 6

Robby didn't wait a whole week to call. He decided he would tell Don that he was just going to mail the money to the church. He had it all in an envelope, addressed and ready to mail. So why didn't he just do it? Why did he have to call? Did he really think that the church would help them?

Things weren't getting any better. But his dad still seemed to find little odd jobs that brought in some extra cash. *Extra cash? You can't have extra of something you don't have enough of in the first place.* It just slowed down the getting worse.

Jack Wilson's unemployment compensation had run out just after Christmas, making things worse yet. They then cancelled their cable service, took one of their cell phones out of service, and dropped the insurance on Jack's truck to save money. "I just won't drive it unless I absolutely have to," Robby heard his dad say to his mother after a lengthy discussion. And it was always cold in their house. He knew that wouldn't last much longer because the weather was changing, but Robby still worried about someone getting sick.

This time Lucy answered the telephone. "Hello," she said.

Robby hesitated and let out a long sigh. "Can I talk to Don?" he asked finally.

"Oh, dear. He's working out on the treadmill. Can I have him call you? He should be done in about a half an hour." Lucy knew who she was talking to and was sure he wouldn't leave his number. They were waiting for his return call. Any young person calling their home would very likely be from Don's Sunday school class and would address Lucy directly.

She had a pleasant, friendly voice, but Robby wasn't going to be charmed into leaving his number. His sisters would be home from school soon, and he didn't know if he would have time to call back today. After another sigh, Robby said, "No, I'll just call back later."

"He plans to be home all evening, so you can call any time. Is this about the Sunday school class?" Don helped teach the high school Sunday school class, so it was a natural question. *Maybe I can get something out of him*, Lucy thought.

"No," Robby said quickly.

"I'm Lucy, his wife. Anything I can help you with?"

"No, thanks." Robby hung up.

"So much for that," said Lucy and put down the phone.

Robby felt betrayed. *He told her. She knew who I was. He said I should trust him. How many other people has he told? The whole church probably knows. Maybe even the police.* "Guess what?" he probably said. "The thief called." Robby didn't know what to do. He wanted to tell Don what he thought of him, for all the good that would do. He tried to calm himself down. His sisters would be home soon, and he didn't know where his dad was. He didn't want him to walk in while he was talking to Don. Why should he call him at all now? Why didn't he just keep the money and forget it? The phone rang.

It was his dad. "Hi, Rob, I'm helping a guy with a plumbing problem and won't be home for another hour or so."

"Okay."

"Everything all right?"

"Yeah."

"You don't sound happy."

"I'm fine. I just got a lot of dumb homework," Robby lied. *I'm getting good at this*, he thought. Just then his sisters stomped in the door.

"You sure?" his dad said.

"Yeah," Robby said again, trying to sound convincing.

"Okay, I'll see you soon."

Robby hung up and turned his attention to his sisters. They were putting their school stuff away but still had their coats on. "We're going over to Melinda's," Cassie announced. "How long can we stay?"

"Dad's doing some job, so dinner will probably be late. You should probably leave when her mom starts getting their dinner ready."

Now Robby was alone and safe from any interruptions. His anger had subsided, but he still wasn't sure what to do. He decided that he was going to tell Don that he wasn't going to fall for his trap and that by telling other people Don had proved to Robby that he couldn't trust him. He waited twenty more minutes and then dialed the phone.

It was the pleasant voice again. "Can I talk to Don?" Robby asked right away this time.

"Oh, hi. He's been waiting for your call. He was afraid you weren't calling back. Here he is."

"Hello," said Don.

"How many people did you tell that I called?" Robby started.

"Whoa, where'd that come from?"

"You told your wife; who else did you tell? You said I would have to trust you," said Robby, still more agitated than he realized.

"What makes you think I told my wife? She thought you were someone from the high school class I help teach at church. It's not that uncommon for a teenager to call here." *If he pushes me, I'll have to confess*, thought Don.

"I could tell she knew. You told her, didn't you?" Robby wasn't so sure anymore.

"Yes, I did." Don spaced the words slowly. "I share all of my problems with her. She helps me sort them out. I have told no one else. You can trust my wife completely. We have an understanding about that. Her name, by the way, is Lucy."

"I know; she told me. How do I know you didn't tell anybody else?" Robby pushed.

"That's where the trust comes in. What have you and your friend decided?"

Robby hesitated. "My friend decided to just mail the money to the church."

"Just money stuffed in an envelope?" Don asked. "Isn't that kind of risky?"

"Why?"

"Someone sorting the mail who sees a bulky envelope with no return address might get curious and open it. Who would ever know? The church isn't expecting it, so they wouldn't know they didn't get it. And you wouldn't know either; they're not going to send you a thank-you note. Or maybe with that many bills it would be too heavy for standard postage, and with no return address, they would just discard it."

"You're just trying to complicate things." Robby wondered if any of that was possible.

"We can make it simple. Just pick a place to meet, and we'll take care of it that way," Don offered.

"My friend would never do it that way."

"Would you?"

"What do you mean?"

"If you were the one who took the quarters, would you agree to meet with me to give the money back?"

"How would I know? What does that matter?"

"Well, when we started this conversation, you were upset that I had betrayed your trust. You didn't come right out and call me a liar, but you were close. So how honest are you being with me? I don't believe there is a friend. Neither does Lucy. People just feel safer saying they're asking for a friend. That way they don't have to expose themselves. Is there a friend or not?" Don anticipated a hang-up.

Robby was trapped. He started to hang up, but he didn't. He was tired of lying, tired of the burden of the whole thing. "No," he said finally. "Is that how you figured it out?"

"That and the feeling in your voice when you told me about your family's problems. So where do you want to meet?"

"I can't. My family would be so embarrassed. I can't do that to them."

"You're going to meet with me, not your family. The only way your family will find out is if you tell them. If I were your father, I would absolutely disapprove of what you have done and be very disappointed that you did it, but I would be so proud that you cared so much about your family that you would take that kind of personal risk. And I wouldn't love you any less." Robby was close to tears and did not respond.

"I can tell that you care a lot about your family," Don went on, "and I would like to help you if you'll let me. My church can't fix your situation, but we can help you get by until it does get fixed. I know there are people in my church who would do everything in their power to make sure you didn't lose your house or that you would get proper medical attention if someone got seriously ill. Those are the things you seem most concerned about." Don waited for some kind of response. "So how about it?" he coaxed. "Do you want to think it over and call me back?"

Robby knew he had to do it. "Yes," he said softly and hung up.

Don slowly hung up the phone, wondering if he would ever hear from the young boy again. There was a lot for him to sort out. *Whether he meets with me or not,* thought Don, *his conscience is going to drive him to tell his parents. I wonder if that's his biggest fear.*

"How'd it go?" Lucy called from the kitchen.

"He was pretty upset. He confessed that there was no friend. I really think there's a chance that I'll get to meet him."

"That's what you want to happen. Don't get your hopes up."

"My hopes are up. We'll just keep praying that God keeps nudging him."

Robby sprawled across his bed, thinking about his conversation with Don. Could his dad actually be proud of him after knowing that he was a thief? That's how he thought of himself. And what about this God thing Don had talked about before? He didn't really know anything about God. Could God make him do something wrong so his family would get help? That didn't make any sense. He decided he would call Don tomorrow.

CHAPTER 7

Robby leaned against his bike at the side of the Taco Bell out of the wind. It was farther than he wanted to go, but he didn't want to be seen by anyone who knew him. They had agreed that Don would meet him there. Even though he was nervous, he was sure he was doing the right thing. He just wanted to get rid of the money.

A red van pulled into the far end of the parking lot. *I hope that's him*, thought Robby. *I'm not sure I'll recognize him; I only saw him that one time at church.* The van stopped beside him, and the window rolled down. "Robby?" asked Don.

"Yeah," Robby said nervously.

Don stuck out his hand. "I'm glad to finally get to meet you."

Robby shook his hand. "Yeah, me too" was all he could think to say.

"Let me get parked and we'll go inside out of the cold."

"Okay" said Robby. "Oh, here," he said, pulling the money envelope from inside his coat.

"You didn't keep any of it did you?" Don said sternly, casually tossing it on the dashboard.

"No! It's all—" Robby started to protest then saw that Don was smiling and realized that he was teasing him.

"I'll tell you, Robby, if you're going to be serious all the time, we're not going to get along very well."

"Okay." Robby laughed, feeling a little better.

Don parked the van and they went inside. Robby ordered a burrito and a Pepsi. Don had a Diet Pepsi. "Are you sure that's all you want?" Don asked.

"Yeah," said Robby unconvincingly. It wasn't. He went back later and got a large order of nachos.

"I don't want to spend a lot of time on this money thing, so let's get it out of the way first," said Don. "I can make up any number of ways how the money was returned anonymously, but I think it's important for the church to know that someone had a change of heart. Do you want to write a note, or do you want me to?"

"What would I say?" Robby asked uneasily.

"Anything that would let the church know you were truly sorry and that you have no defense for doing something that was clearly wrong," said Don. "But don't give any details that would give you away," he added.

Robby took a big bite of his burrito to stall for time. *Is this some kind of punishment?* he wondered. "I'm not sure I can do that," he said.

"Let's do this," said Don, "Let's both write something down and then combine our ideas into something we agree on."

"Now?"

"No. We'll meet again next week to take care of it. It doesn't matter when I turn the money in. We're the only ones who know I have it." Don wanted to have a reason to stay in touch with Robby. "I'll pick you up at the school."

Robby had another mouth full of food, so he just nodded in agreement.

"Okay, now let's talk about what we can do to help your family. My church has all kinds of committees for all kinds of things for all kinds of people, no questions asked, no strings attached. What's your food situation?"

Robby's stomach flip-flopped. He hadn't told Don about taking the food every week. He just sat there. "What's wrong?" asked Don, clearly puzzled.

Robby put down the burrito and buried his face in his hands. "Okay, dude, what's going on? What haven't you told me?" Don could only imagine.

Robby told him about taking the canned goods and the cereal when he came to pick up Cassie. Don just laughed. "Robby, we collect that food for people who need it. All you have to do is ask. Some of our women would send you home with more than you can carry. And make you come back for more. I'll make sure you get stuff every week. How did you keep your parents from finding out?"

Robby told him about eating the cereal in his room and slipping the cans into the cupboard.

"Well, now you can just tell them, and you won't have to hide in your room."

"No," said Robby sadly, shaking his head. "My dad won't accept charity from anyone." He told Don about the food bank conflict between his parents at Christmastime.

"So you're telling me that if we collect some money to help with your mortgage payments, your dad will refuse it."

"That's what I'm telling you."

"Sounds like your dad is a proud man. I can understand that. He's always had a good job, paid his bills, has a great family that looks up to him, and now he feels like he's let them down. He's probably more embarrassed for you and your sisters—and your mother—than he is for himself. He's supposed to take care of you, and he's not doing it. That's a big load to carry around. He probably thinks he's not worth much."

"But he is! He just won't talk to anybody about it." Robby clenched his teeth.

"Robby, what you think of him is very important to him. You need to let him know how you feel about all this and tell him that you know he's doing the best he can," Don said. "And tell him you're proud that he's your dad."

"Why are you doing this?" asked Robby, close to tears. "Why are you trying to help me—us, my family?"

Don thought for a moment. "Well, Robby," he started slowly, "I really believe that God sent you to us. If one morning you found a baby in a basket on your front porch, wouldn't your family do everything you could to help it?"

Robby just shrugged, not sure what Don was getting at.

"I really think that God has plopped you on the doorstep of our church and I got picked to be the one to find you. And I believe that God expects that we will do what we can to help your family through its difficulty. There are many places in the Bible that we are told to help each other. Do you have a Bible at home?"

"I think my mom might have one." Robby wasn't really sure.

"Do either of your parents have any church background?"

"They both went when they were kids but not anymore. My dad was forced to go, and he hated it. I guess there were a lot of fights about it. I heard my mom tell someone my dad said he would never do that to his kids. I think my mom would go to church if my dad wasn't so much against it. Not now, though, because she works so much."

Don thought about all that. "Robby, I want you to talk to your dad about how you feel. Tell him you talked to some old guy from the church while you were waiting for your sister and he told you about the food we give away and offered some of it to you. If he gets upset, just let it go, and we'll try to think of something else. Do not get into an argument."

Robby let out a deep breath. "I'll try," he said. "Oh! What time is it? I have to pick up Cassie."

"It's just four thirty. I gave a girl named Cassie a book to read a few weeks back; is that your sister?"

"Yeah, I read it."

"What did you think?"

"It was a cool story. That's what made me start thinking about giving the money back. That's how I found your address."

They stepped outside and were greeted by swirling snow and a drop in the temperature. "We better throw your bike in the back of the van and I'll take you to the church," said Don. "If it's still snowing this hard, I'll take you and your sister home."

As they pulled into the parking lot, Don said to Robby, "I'm going to sic Jay onto you. He's the best person to help you understand what I've been trying to tell you."

"Is he that after-school guy?"

Don laughed. "He's more than an after-school guy. He's the youth minister for our church. He can get you into more trouble than you can think of yourself. Well, maybe not you," Don added, smiling. Robby gave him a sour look as they went through the door.

They went back into the gym just as the program was finishing up. Don took Robby over to Jay. "Jay, I'd like you to meet a friend of mine."

"You mean Cassie's brother?" said Jay.

"Showoff," said Don.

"Hey, he picks her up every week, and I remember him from last year."

"Showoff," Don said again.

"How are you, Robby?" said Jay, offering his hand and completely ignoring Don.

"I'm fine," answered Robby, enjoying the verbal jousting between the two friends.

"Robby and I have been having some conversations about God messing around in our lives, and I told him that I was going to turn him over to you," Don said to Jay.

"Does that mean you have him thoroughly confused?"

"Pretty much. And I know you can make sure he stays that way."

"We're really good friends," said Jay, turning to a grinning Robby. "We just don't want anybody to know it."

Just then Don spied Cassie across the room. "I'll let you two chat. I want to find out how Cassie liked that book I gave her."

"Hi, Cassie," said Don as he walked up to a small group of girls saying good-bye to each other.

"Oh, hi," she said, smiling.

"I haven't seen you since I gave you the book. Thanks for returning it promptly. Did you like it?" asked Don.

"Yes, I read it twice. Well, actually once. My little sister read it to the whole family, so I read it once and heard it once."

I'll bet Robby did some squirming through that, thought Don. "Did your family enjoy it?"

"Yes, and I told them about the video too." Cassie acted like she wanted to say something else but thought better of it.

"What?" asked Don.

"Well," Cassie started. "Nothing."

"What is it?"

"My sister told her teacher about the book, and the teacher asked her if she could bring it in, but my mom said she couldn't because it wasn't my book. I thought you wouldn't care, but my parents said we needed permission, so she didn't take it."

"I understand why your parents said what they did. But you were right; I wouldn't care. In fact I would be most pleased to have your sister's class hear the story. The more people who hear it, the more support for Heifer. I want you to tell your sister to find out if her teacher would still like to have the book, and if she does, call me and I will bring it to your house. Okay?"

"Megan would like that." Cassie smiled.

"Like what?" asked Robby, who just caught the tail end of their conversation.

"To take *Beatrice's Goat* to school. Don's going to bring it to her," announced Cassie.

Don and Robby exchanged glances as the three of them headed toward the parking lot. "What did you and Jay talk about?" Don asked Robby.

"He wants me to come to the Sunday night high school youth program."

"Are you going to?" asked Don.

"I don't know. I told him I'd think about it."

"If you do, I could go to the junior high one. My friends have been asking me to go." Cassie chimed in.

"Sounds like a plan to me," said Don, pushing the door open. The ding-dong of the alarm gave Robby a shiver. "Come on; I'll give you a ride home," he offered.

On the way to their house, Don had Cassie write down his phone number so she could call him about the book. *I could have told her that*, said Robby to himself. "Have Megan call me if she wants the book," Don said as he dropped them off in front of their house.

"Okay, bye, thanks," they both shouted as they ran into the house.

CHAPTER 8

"Hi, Don. It's Cassie."

"Hi, Cassie. How are you?" said Don.

"Fine, thanks. I'm calling for Megan. She's too shy. She wants the book."

"Is she right there?"

"Yes."

"I have some questions I would like to ask her. See if she'll talk to me."

Don could hear an animated conversation in the background. He couldn't make out the words but could tell that Cassie was being persistent. "Hello," said a tiny voice.

"Hello, Megan," said Don. "Cassie told me you would like to borrow *Beatrice's Goat* to take to school."

"My teacher wants to read it to the class." Don could barely hear her.

"What time do you get home from school?"

"We get out at three thirty." Megan's voice was getting bigger.

"What if I bring the book over tomorrow around four o'clock? Would that be okay?"

He heard her say some muffled words to whoever was there with her. "It's okay. Robby will be here," she said.

"Fine," said Don. "I'll see you tomorrow." *One more step*, Don thought as he hung up.

Cassie answered the door with her usual exuberance. Megan shyly shook Don's hand and quickly sat down across the room. Robby sort of waved from the kitchen doorway. Don had brought some pictures of a trip that he and Lucy had taken with a Heifer group to Honduras, hoping he could show them to Megan and her siblings. He was barely inside the door and couldn't decide whether he had been invited in or not. *Give it a shot*, he said to himself and walked over to Megan.

"Here's the book, Megan. You tell your teacher that she may share it with other teachers if they want to read it to their classes."

"What do you say, Megan?" prompted Robby, stepping out of the doorway.

"Thank you," she said in her tiny voice, her eyes fixed on the book.

"You're welcome, Megan. I hope your class likes the story as much as you did."

Don pulled the pictures from his coat pocket. "I have some pictures from a Heifer trip that my wife and I went on to Honduras. Would you be interested in seeing them?" Don asked, not at all sure what the answer would be.

Cassie took them from him and started sorting through them. "Sure," said Robby and sat down on the couch. Cassie handed him back the pictures and sat down also, leaving a small space between her and her brother. Don draped his coat over a chair and wedged himself between them in front of the coffee table. To his surprise, Megan came over and sat on the floor across the table from him.

"We visited several projects like the one they tell about in *Beatrice's Goat*. Most of these pictures are of a family we met that is being helped by Heifer," Don started, showing them a picture of a family of five standing in front of a gray wall—a mother, father, two girls about the same age as Cassie and Megan, and a five- or six-year-old boy. Other pictures showed a room with concrete walls filled with beds, boxes, and clothes spread all around.

"Is that their bedroom?" asked Cassie with a sour look on her face.

"No," said Don. "That's their home."

"What!" exclaimed Robby, suddenly interested, as he took a closer look.

"That's their home. It's all they have. It's an old, abandoned cistern that they cut a hole in the side for a door. Everything they own you see in those pictures."

"What's a cistern?" asked Cassie.

"It's a big tank for collecting rainwater. This one is a large concrete box built by a rich landowner. They ran pipes from the roofs of houses and other buildings to collect water so they wouldn't have to go to the river to get it. The owner tore the houses down and built a new one somewhere else where there was running water. They left the cistern as it was, so Anival moved his family into it."

They were all three looking on the backs of the photographs where the names of the family were written. "They stay in that box all day?" Robby asked in disbelief.

"Well, they mostly live outside. They only sleep in the cistern. Unless it's raining," Don explained.

"Where do they sit?" Megan wanted to know.

"On the ground or on those big rocks you see scattered around. You see in this picture what we would call an outdoor barbeque. Anival added it on the outside so his wife would have a place to cook."

"They cook their food there?" asked Cassie.

"Yes."

"All of it?"

"All of it. It's their kitchen."

"That hammock is kind of cool," said Robby, referring to the younger girl posing in a hammock to get her picture taken.

"That's Maria. I was lucky enough to get her picture when she was smiling. The hammock is one of their beds. It's crowded and hot in the cistern, so they take turns sleeping outside." Don noticed that Robby couldn't stop shaking his head.

"What's this?" asked Megan, showing Don a picture of a cluster of watermelon-sized rocks covered partially with a blue cloth that had stuffed bear laying on it.

"I asked that same question," said Don. "That bear is Maria's only toy. She was playing some pretend game with it, and that was the best place she could find for a bed for her little bear friend."

"Did she tell you that?"

"Sort of. She explained it all very carefully to the interpreter, and he told us what she said."

Just then a door in the rear of the house opened. "It's Daddy!" exclaimed Megan, grabbing the book and running into the kitchen with Cassie close on her heels.

"I haven't talked to him yet," Robby said quickly. Don gave him a shrug of understanding.

"Look! Don brought me the book," Don heard Megan say.

"He's been telling us about poor people in Honduras," said Cassie.

"Let me put these groceries down, and then you can tell me all about it," Jack said.

Not wanting to wait, Megan announced in her most important voice, "They live in a cistern."

"Okay, that's interesting." Jack chuckled.

"They really do, Dad," said Cassie. "It's awful. You should see the pictures."

"I'm sure I will," said Jack, coming out into the living room.

Don stood up and stuck out his hand. "I'm Don," he said. "I've been enjoying your children."

"I'm Jack," he responded, shaking Don's hand. "I've been hearing a lot about you." His tone of voice was unreadable.

"See, Dad. Look at this. This is where they live." Cassie held the pictures of the inside of the cistern in front of her father's face.

"And the girl that's my age has to sleep in a hammock and has to use big rocks for a pretend bed for her bear," chimed in Megan, handing Jack more pictures before he could look at the ones Cassie gave him.

Jack looked at the pictures without saying anything. Don noticed that Robby had become very uneasy. "Well," said Jack, continuing to sort through the pictures, "it looks like you guys are rich." There was a trace of sarcasm in his voice.

After an uncomfortable silence, Don said, "I think we're all rich compared to people living in those conditions."

"Is that why you showed my kids these pictures?" said Jack, his voice clearly strained. "So they wouldn't think they were poor?"

"Dad!" Robby started, but Don held up his hand to stop him.

"I take advantage of every opportunity I have to tell these stories. To anyone and everyone I can," Don said carefully. "I have done so with your children because they showed an interest. It has nothing to do with them being poor, whatever you meant by that. It looks like you're doing pretty well to me," said Don, glancing around the pleasant, well-kept room as he went to get his coat.

"Have you ever been out of a job?" Jack continued the attack.

"No."

"Do you have any idea what it's like to be out of a job for nine months and not be able to find another one?"

"I can only imagine," said Don. "I probably wouldn't deal with it very well."

"Like I'm not right now?" Jack spat out. "Because someone thinks it's his job to tell my kids they're not as bad off as some other kids so they won't feel bad because they're poor." Jack threw the pictures down on the coffee table, some of them spilling onto the floor.

Megan scurried to pick them up and handed all of them to Don. Then she handed the book up to Don. "I don't have to take *Beatrice's Goat* to school," she said, the sadness in her voice mirroring the sadness on her face.

"I'm honored that you would want to share my book with your classmates, Megan," said Don, gently pushing the book to her chest and folding her arms across it. "Please don't change your mind."

"Have you ever been poor?" Jack started in again. "Have you ever had to worry if you were going to have enough food or if you were going to be able to make your next house payment? Have you ever not been able to buy your kids presents for Christmas?"

Robby couldn't believe he was hearing his father say these things. He had never told them he had those worries. Now Robby was more worried than ever. Cassie was curled up at the end of the couch, softly crying. Megan sat cross-legged on the floor, looking sadder than ever.

Don had started to put on his coat before Jack's last outburst. He paused, trying to decide how to answer all that, wondering if he even should. He took a step toward the door and then stopped. He sat down in the nearest chair and looked squarely at Jack.

"When I was about eleven years old, just before Thanksgiving, my dad got sick. They figured out that he had some form of rheumatoid arthritis. He had a high fever, and his whole body was racked with pain. There was no such thing as medical insurance, so he couldn't stay in the hospital. And no unemployment compensation. Somehow my mother was able to get a hospital bed that we put in my baby brother's bedroom and moved him in with her. Every day we would take turns sitting with my dad, cranking the bed to whatever position made him more comfortable. Each position change would give him relief for no more than five or ten minutes.

"Night after night we watched him suffer, listened to him moan, out of his head from the fever. Then the fever would break momentarily, and the sheets would be soaked with sweat. That went on until early spring when he started to get better, but he wasn't able to get out of bed until just after Easter. We watched him change from a robust, healthy man into a skeleton with skin. We watched his hair turn gray and then most of it fall out.

"For Christmas that year all I got was an ink pen. My birthday is in January, and all I got for that was a promise. I had really wanted a radio for my room for Christmas, and that got shoved to my birthday. Then the promise that I would get it when there was money. I got the radio in June. It was on of the most treasured gifts I have ever received."

Don paused and took a deep breath. "I don't know how my mother held it together, but she did. I remember that she rented out one of our bedrooms to a young married couple for a while and I had to share a room with my other brother. I was never told who helped us through that, but money had to come from somewhere. I do remember baskets and boxes of food being left on our porch. Nobody ever brought anything to the door; the stuff just showed up on the porch."

Don stood up to go. "When people are going through a hard time, they have to let others help them. Then when things get better they can help somebody else. There is always someone who is having some kind of struggle. You might want to think about that. I hope I've answered your question. Stay happy, kids." And he went out the door.

After Don left, no one said anything. Jack went into the kitchen to start dinner. The girls went to their room, but Robby just stayed there slumped on the couch. After a while he got up and walked back to his room. He lay there on his bed trying to figure out how he could ever talk to his dad like Don said he should. Maybe Don would understand now why he was afraid to say anything.

Robby thought about Don's dad, how he had changed so much right before Don's eyes. His dad wasn't sick, but he had changed right before his eyes. *When is he going to get better?* Robby decided he would ask Don that question on Wednesday.

The four of them ate dinner in silence. Jack had to go back to Cassie's room twice before she would come out. Robby ate quickly and then excused himself. The girls picked at their food for a while and then scraped their plates off in the sink, put them in the dishwasher, and went back to their room. Sally was scheduled to work until seven, so Jack made up a plate for her to heat up when she got home.

Jack was still cleaning up in the kitchen when Sally came in the back door. "Hi," she said, smiling and giving him a kiss.

"Hi," said Jack, continuing to wipe off the counter and not smiling.

"What's wrong?" asked Sally, taking off her coat.

"Nothing."

"Where are the kids?" Sally was used to being greeted by her whole family when she came home.

"They're all in their rooms hating their father," Don said, taking Sally's dinner out of the microwave.

"You're not going to tell me what happened?"

Jack stood leaning against the counter with his arms crossed, looking down at the floor. "That guy brought the book over that Megan is so excited about. When I got here he was showing them pictures of some poor family in some county where he'd been."

"So?" Sally waited for him to continue.

"I don't know this guy. He's someone from that church Cassie goes to. Now Robby's going over there on Sunday night. I know what those people are like. I don't want them influencing my kids."

"Did you talk to him?"

"Yeah." Jack looked away again.

"Pleasantly?" Sally didn't want to hear the answer.

"No," he answered, looking up at her.

"What did you say?" Sally sighed.

"I don't know what set me off, but I ended up accusing him of showing the kids those pictures so they wouldn't feel so bad about being poor," Jack confessed. "Then I said a bunch of other stuff."

"Like what?"

"Like he didn't know what it was like to not be able to buy your kids Christmas presents or to worry about not being able to pay the mortgage, and all the rest of it. It just all came out."

Neither of them spoke for a while. "I embarrassed my kids, Sally," Jack said finally.

"You know, Jack, the kids like that man," Sally said softly. "Cassie says all the people at the church are so friendly to her. She says everybody knows who she is. She likes to be there, Jack. You need to think about that."

That's what that Don guy said to me. Jack recalled Don's words as he left. "Maybe I need to think about a lot of things," he said, mostly to himself.

"I had my hours changed to one to five on Sundays," Sally said quietly.

"Okay. Why? What's that got to do with anything?"

"That way I can go to church with my kids. We should both go."

Jack unfolded his arms, pushed away from the counter, went into the living room, and turned on the TV, leaving Sally to finish her dinner alone.

After she finished her dinner, Sally knocked on Robby's door, getting no response. She pushed it open and stuck her head in. "May I come in?" she asked carefully.

"Oh, hi, Mom," Robby said softly.

She took that as a yes and went in and sat on the edge of his bed. "Do you want to talk?"

"Not really."

"Well, I do," said Sally, getting a trace of a smile from Robby and letting him know he didn't have a choice. "I guess your dad blew it this afternoon."

"He said that?" Robby was surprised.

"He didn't exactly say that, but I could tell he thinks he did. Part of it is his problem with church, and part of it is the worry about not having a job. He's under a lot of stress."

"So am I, but I don't go around yelling ugly things at people."

"It's different when you're an adult."

"No! It's different when you're a kid. Adults can say whatever they want. I'd be in big trouble if I said stuff like that." Robby was angry.

Sally didn't speak for a while. "Well, he is in trouble."

"With who?" Robby was confused.

"With you and your sisters," she answered. "And with me."

"I don't want you to fight." Robby was alarmed.

"We're not going to fight." His mother smiled. "But we're going to have an understanding about this church thing," she said with more confidence than she felt. Robby just looked at her.

"I've had my Sunday hours changed so we can all go to church together," she went on.

"Did you tell Dad?"

"Yes. And I invited him to come with us."

"I'm sure he'll go," said Robby sarcastically.

"Probably not," Sally said understandingly, "but I want us to start going."

"Me too," said Robby. "I like that youth minister guy." Robby suddenly wanted to tell his mother about the quarters. *Not now*, he said to himself.

"Okay, it's a deal," said Sally, getting up. "I've got one more stop to make. Do you feel better now?"

"Not that much," he said honestly. Sally kissed him on the forehead and headed toward her daughters' room.

"Hi, girls," she said as she walked in without knocking. "I've just talked to Robby about what went on this afternoon. What do you guys have to say?"

"Daddy was mean to Don," Megan piped up.

"Why couldn't he just be nice?" asked Cassie. "Did Robby tell you what he said?"

"No, but your dad did."

"He told you?" they asked in unison.

"Yes. And I don't think he's very happy with himself."

"I'm not very happy with him either." Megan scowled.

"Well, your dad's going through a very hard time that's not easy for you to understand, but we all have to get along. Even though your dad made a mistake today, you can't stay mad at him. Give him some time to think about it, and I'm sure he'll talk to you about it. I gave him something else to think about tonight that didn't exactly please him."

"What?" they said.

"I have changed my Sunday hours so we can all go to church together. But it doesn't start this week because I was already scheduled for this Sunday."

"Daddy too?" asked Megan.

"Not right now. That's probably going to take some work," Sally answered, wondering if it could ever be possible.

"I'm glad you did that, Mom. It makes me feel good," said Cassie, giving her a hug.

Jack, meanwhile, was having a talk of his own. With himself. *How could I be such an idiot? That man knows exactly what we're going through. Only, none of us is sick. His dad had a job waiting for him, though. I can't even get anybody to talk to me. And more people are getting laid off every day. What chance do I have?*

Jack realized that part of his reaction to Don came from his feelings about the church. His recollections were of an angry, scowling man shouting from the pulpit that everything bad that happened to you was because you were a terrible sinner and God was going to punish you for it. And that threat was repeated constantly at home. He rebelled against going to church as a teenager and never went at all after he left home. He got a job at the factory as soon as he graduated from high school and immediately moved into an apartment. A few years later, Jack's father accepted a company transfer to Illinois, and they had little to do with each other after that.

He and Sally met while she was in college, and they soon decided to get married. They were married in Sally's church, at the insistence of her parents. At first Sally would go off and on by herself but then gave it up altogether. Then she got pregnant and dropped out of college. She stayed at home and raised her children until Megan was in first grade and then took the job at Walmart. Sally was a late-in-life, only child, the last attempt of two people who had suffered through three miscarriages. She had watched both of her parents and all of their money waste away in a nursing home. Funeral expenses had taken a toll on what savings they had accumulated. Robby, Cassie, and Megan had never known any of their grandparents. They had visited Illinois a few times over the years, and the kids got the same church treatment that Jack had when he was young.

Maybe that's why they like this Don guy, thought Jack. *I wonder if he has grandkids. He doesn't seem like the church people I remember. And Cassie says everyone is friendly to her. I don't remember anyone ever being friendly to me. Can it be that much different? Why did I say those things? Now I have to patch things up with the kids. If they'll let me.*

Just then Sally came into the room and sat beside him on the couch. There was a basketball game on the TV, but Jack had muted it. He didn't even know who was playing. Sally took the remote from his hand and replaced it with hers. He took the remote back from her with his other hand and clicked the TV off.

"Your kids are unhappy with you," Sally said softly.

"Who could blame them?"

"Not me."

"Me either."

"How are you going to fix it?"

Jack just sighed. "You have to fix it," Sally said, not so softly now.

"I will," he said, putting his arm around her and pulling her close.

CHAPTER 9

The next Wednesday Robby was pacing up and down along the sidewalk in front of the school, waiting for Don. It was a cool, late-March day, but the sun felt good. It didn't do much to lift his spirits, though. He was sure Don wouldn't show up for their meeting. Why should he after the way his dad had treated him? Robby had hardly spoken to his dad since last Friday. He spent as much time as he could away from the house over the weekend, and when he was home he stayed mostly in his room. "Are you punishing your father or yourself?" his mother had asked him.

He wasn't exactly sure. Was he avoiding his dad because he was mad at him or because he was putting off the talk Don said he should have with him? It was as though he and his dad had become strangers. And not just because of last Friday. Jack had always helped coach Robby's Little League teams and was always there when he tried to run track in middle school. Everything Robby ever did, his dad was always there. Now his dad rarely even asked him about his schoolwork. He did talk to him that one time about the snow-shoveling money. Why was that such a big deal?

Robby knew his dad had never stopped looking for a job. He knew that Jack had started looking even before the plant closed, hoping to find something before he was out of work. Robby couldn't imagine how many résumés and letters his dad had sent out. Or how many phone calls. It seemed like hundreds.

It scared Robby when he thought of how close he came to telling his mother about the quarters. That was something his dad didn't need to know about right now. Or his mom. But he wanted to tell her, and he couldn't understand why. He stood by the curb, his hands bunched in his pockets, ready to give up and go home, when he saw Don's red van turn in from the street.

When Don pulled onto the school grounds, he wondered if Robby would even show up. He had, in fact, been wondering that since his visit to Robby's house the Friday before. But there he was, all 125 pounds of him, standing next to the curb, slumped down with his hands in his pockets. *How much fun is this going to be?* thought Don.

"Hi, Robby," said Don cheerfully as Robby climbed in.

"Hello," said Robby dejectedly, staring straight ahead.

"Why so happy?" asked Don.

Robby tried hard not to smile and almost made it. He was feeling better already. "I didn't think you'd come."

"I didn't think you'd be here."

"Why?"

"That's my question to you," said Don.

"I thought because my dad ... " Robby folded his arms across his chest and slumped farther down in the seat.

"Because your dad took his frustrations out on me and embarrassed you and you sisters?" Don finished for him.

"Duh."

"Hey, I can be pretty smart sometimes." Don smiled.

Robby suppressed a smile of his own and maintained his silence. "Have you forgiven him?" Don asked.

"I don't know," Robby muttered.

"Have you?" Don asked again, looking over at him.

"I really don't know. Why should I have to forgive him? He's my dad."

"Well, you can't be mad at him the rest of your life," said Don as he eased the van into a parking spot at Taco Bell.

"I'm not mad at him. I just don't understand why... anything," Robby said, slamming the van door in frustration.

Neither spoke until they got their food and found a booth away from the other customers. "I almost told my mom about the quarters," Robby broke the silence.

"Oops," said Don.

"Yeah, I know. I want to tell them, but I'm afraid to. I'm so mixed up I don't say anything. To my dad, anyway."

"Well, Robby, you are going to have to tell them sometime, but I don't think now is the time. You're carrying around a great burden that you need to get rid of, but you can't pile it on top of what your parents are already dealing with. Your dad is a pretty intense guy who's not feeling very good about himself. He thinks he's letting his family down, and in spite of all of his efforts, he can't change that right now. And he's letting his pride get in the way."

"I don't think he's a failure. I know how hard he's trying to get a job," Robby protested.

"Does he know that's what you think? That's why you need to talk to him. He needs to know that. You seem to be able to talk to your mom. I'd like to meet her."

"You probably will," said Robby enigmatically.

"I'm waiting."

"She had her hours changed so we could all go to church together." Robby smiled.

Awesome, thought Don. *I can't believe Jack will be with them.* "Does that mean I'll see you in my Sunday school class?" Don asked, deciding not to ask about Jack.

"Probably. I had fun Sunday night."

"No pressure?"

"No, it was all cool. They talked a lot about the work mission."

"Does that interest you?" asked Don.

Robby hesitated. "Yeah, kind of."

"Go."

"What do you mean?"

"Go on the work mission. When we go back to get Cassie, tell Jay you're going."

"I don't have the money."

"It's already paid for," said Don.

"How?" Robby was confused.

"There's a fund for those want to go but can't come up with all or any of the money. No one who wants to go gets left out," Don explained.

"One more thing to freak my dad out."

"One more reason to have that talk with him," said Don.

Robby didn't respond, so Don decided to let that go for the time being. "What did you come up with for a note to put with the money when I turn it in?" he asked.

"I've thought about some stuff, but I didn't write anything down," Robby said sheepishly, stuffing the last of a taco in his mouth.

"Tell me the stuff you thought about," Don pressed him.

Robby took his time chewing his food before answering. "I'm sorry I did it. I knew it was wrong. I wish I hadn't done it. I hope everybody doesn't hate me," Robby recited. "I just don't know any other way to say it," he added sadly.

"How about something like, 'I took the money because I thought it would help me over a rough spot. After I found out what it was for, I didn't like myself very much and decided to give it back. I'm sorry. I hope you'll forgive me'?" Don suggested.

"How can they forgive me? They don't even know who I am."

"The point is, they already have. Most of the people I've talked to about it just hope that it helped whoever took it."

"So I stole it, but I gave it back. Is that like unstealing it and it doesn't count and I don't have to be forgiven?" said Robby.

"Nice try." Don laughed. "First you have to understand that they forgave you before you 'unstole' the money, so your argument won't work. It looks to me like you're having trouble forgiving yourself."

"I just don't like what it's going to do to my family when they find out. My dad will probably say it's his fault because I wouldn't have done it if he had a job."

"But that's true, isn't it?"

"Yes, it is. But it's not his fault, it's mine!" Robby put his head in his hands and stared down at the table.

"Let's pray about it this week, and then we'll talk about it again next Wednesday," said Don.

"I don't know how to pray," Robby said to the table.

"Just pour your heart out to God. Tell him how you feel. Don't leave anything out. Try it; you'll like it." Don got up to leave. "We better get you over to the church."

The drive to the church was done in silence. Robby trudged up the walk and into the church. He perked up a little when Don gave him a pat on the back and gently pushed him ahead through the door into the gym. Cassie saw Robby and started over to him. Then she saw Don and turned to join a group of kids talking off to the side of the gym. Robby looked at Don and shrugged. Don walked over to the group. He knew two of them. "Hi, Courtney. Hi, Tony," Don greeted them, getting a "Hi, Don" and a hug from Courtney and a high-five from Tony.

"I don't know your friends," he said, standing right beside Cassie.

They introduced him to everyone, and then Courtney said, "You know Cassie, don't you?"

"Sort of." Don smiled and gave her a little hip bump.

Cassie bit her lip, started to turn away, and then turned back, gave him a hug, and buried her face in his coat. The other kids gave them puzzled looks but didn't say anything.

"There has been a misunderstanding, and Cassie is just happy that it's been straightened out," Don explained, not sure what to do next.

"What happened?" asked Courtney.

"Well, something weird happened," said Don, choosing his words carefully, "and Cassie mistakenly thought that I was upset with her. But I don't think she'll ever make that mistake again. Right, Cassie?" Cassie shook her head with her face still buried in Don's coat.

Don waved the others away and stood there holding Cassie, waiting for her to settle down. He tried to ease her away, but she just held him tighter. Don saw that Jay had Robby cornered on the other side of the gym. *How am I going to get out of this?* he thought.

After a while Don said, "Are you getting snot all over my coat?"

Cassie let out a muffled giggle and nodded her head yes. She stepped back, wiping her eyes, still giggling. "Have you been worrying over that since Friday?" Don asked. Cassie nodded and continued to wipe the tears off her face and onto her sleeve.

Don gave her another hug and then steered her over toward Robby and Jay. "My dad was so mean to you," said Cassie.

"He wasn't being mean to me; he just let his frustrations show. He feels like he's not taking care of his family like he should."

"But he doesn't have to yell at you," groused Cassie.

"I didn't think I was being yelled at." Don smiled. "I just wish I could do something to help him."

They stopped a polite distance from Robby and Jay, not wanting to interrupt their conversation. "I just heard something exciting," said Don.

"What?"

"That your mother is coming to church with you Sunday."

"She is." Cassie grinned. "And Megan is coming too. I checked out her Sunday school class and told her the names of some kids she knows."

"You're a good big sister to do that," Don complimented her, getting a big smile in reward of his effort.

"What about my mom?"

"For Sunday school? Don't worry; Lucy will take care of that."

Jay and Robby broke off their conversation and walked over to them. "Robby tells me that you have been harassing him," Jay said to Don.

Don looked at Robby, who just shrugged and tried to look innocent. "What did you tell him to do?" Don asked Jay, figuring out that he was talking about the work mission.

"Pretty much what you did." Jay grinned. "But that he should be sure he wants to go."

"Are you going to think about it?" Don asked Robby.

"Yeah. And talk to my dad," he said seriously, looking at Jay.

He must have talked to Jay about his dad, thought Don. *I need to tell Jay about the prayer conversation. We're making progress.* "Pick a good time," Don advised. "And don't forget to listen."

Later that evening Don was puzzling over what to write in the note he would put with the money Robby had returned. He had decided that he would probably never get Robby to do it. There was a church council meeting the next night, and he wanted to present it to them. When he told the story of the missing quarters at the last meeting, there was a mixture of reactions ranging from "You've got to be kidding" to "What do you expect these days?" But the group as a whole held out the hope that whoever took the money did so because they were in some kind of need. Don had pointed out that there was no after-school program that week because school had been snowed out on Wednesday. His goal had been to deflect any suspicion that someone from that group had been the culprit. Some people in the church had reservations about "all those kids running all over the church." *Turns out that program is indirectly the cause of the money being taken,* he mused.

Don sat back and read through what he hoped was his final draft. Satisfied, he then tackled the problem of writing it in such a way that it didn't look like a young person had written it. He judged his second try acceptable and put it in the envelope with the money, hoping that getting the money returned to the church would relieve some of Robby's burden.

Near the end of the meeting, the chairwoman asked if there was any other business, and Don raised his hand. "Last meeting I told you all about the Heifer quarters being stolen," he started. "This morning I stopped by the church to put a new Heifer magazine on the table and saw that several of them had accumulated there. I started to sort through to remove the older issues when I discovered this envelope." He held the envelope up for all to see. "In it was fifty-eight dollars and twenty-five cents and this note."

Don unfolded the note and read it to them. "Here is your money back. I took it because I needed it. Then I found out what the money was for and felt so bad that I am returning it. I'm sorry. What I did was wrong. I'll get by somehow. I hope you can forgive me."

The room was silent. "Wow," someone softly said finally.

Then someone else asked, "No signature?"

"Just what I read," answered Don.

"We need to know who it is so we can help them." Every head nodded in agreement.

"Unless they come forward, we will never know," said Don, wanting very much to tell them.

"What if we put an article in the newsletter offering them help? They must be connected to the church in some way."

That kicked off a long discussion resulting in Don agreeing to write a thank-you note for the return of the money to be put in the church newsletter along with an offer of whatever kind of assistance that person might need. The offer was to state that only one church member would know the person's identity and all assistance would be funneled through them. Don was pleased with the council's response. *This can work*, he thought, *if only Robby can get through to his dad.*

CHAPTER 10

Sally fussed with her hair for the third time, still not satisfied with the way it looked. *Why am I so worried about the way I look?* she asked herself. It was the same question Cassie had asked her when she was trying to decide what to wear. "I've never noticed anyone wearing fancy clothes. All your stuff looks nice," Cassie had said to her. *Like she would notice*, thought Sally. The truth was Sally didn't have any clothes that she thought were at all fancy.

Sally remembered thinking when she was a child that the women at her parents' church were always very dressed up, hats and all. And the men all wore suits and ties. The last few times she had gone to church after she and Jack were married she had noticed that quite a few men didn't wear ties or even sport coats. Her dad would never have set foot in church on Sunday unless he was wearing a suit and tie. Was all that why she was nervous?

Sally's memories of church were that it was full of stuffy old people. There were very few kids and no one close to her age. There were no activities like Cassie and Robby were involved in. *Cassie tells how friendly everyone is to her.* Sally couldn't remember anyone even noticing that she was there.

"Mom! We're going to be late," Cassie called from the living room. Sally gave one last fluff to her hair and joined her children going out the front door after kissing Jack good-bye.

Sally and Jack had had an uncontentious talk about her going to church the night before. "Jack, there has to be something good going on, or the kids wouldn't want to keep going back," she said. "I want to see for myself what the attraction is. I'd think you would be curious too."

"Sally, you know how I hated going to church. And why."

"I do know; I've heard it enough times, but that doesn't mean that this church is like that. I didn't really like going to church either, but I didn't hate it. It was boring and unfriendly, but no one was mean to me like you say they were to you."

"All I remember is mean-faced old women asking me if I'd been good during the week and telling me it wouldn't do any good to lie because God knew and would punish me anyway. All I ever heard was how bad I was and if I didn't straighten up, I was going to hell. My parents would just stand there and not say a word. If anyone would say something like that to my kids, they'd find out what hell was really like. So I decided I was already there and wanted to be somewhere else, so as soon as I could, I stopped going and left home. And I am in a better place," Jack added, smiling at her.

Sally smiled back, appreciating the sentiment. "I look at some of the papers Cassie brings home, and they all seem to be about love and forgiveness and Jesus healing people. Not what you're talking about or what I remember. The preacher always used such big words I had no idea what he was talking about."

Sally had extracted a promise from him that if she had a good experience he would consider giving it a try. But she wondered if he ever would.

They parked toward the back of the parking lot. Sally had always dropped Cassie off at the door and had never noticed how many cars there were. As they headed toward the door Sally's nervousness started to return. They were greeted at the curb by a friendly young man who called Cassie by name. "See?" said Cassie.

They went up the walk, through the doors, and were greeted again by an older couple. Megan kept Sally between her and the greeters so she wouldn't have to shake hands. She had done that successfully out at the curb. She didn't get away with it this time.

"Is someone too shy to shake my hand?" The woman peered around Sally at Megan.

"Megan isn't shy; she's just checking you out," said a voice over by the coat rack.

Megan turned and ran over to Don. "That's my mom," she exclaimed, pointing to Sally.

Cassie gave Don a hug, and he and Robby gave each other a fist bump. Don then extended his hand to Sally. "Hi, I'm Don. You have great kids," he said to her.

"Thank you," said Sally, shaking his hand. "They feel the same way about you."

Don turned to Megan. "You have to shake hands with my friends Shirley and Dave, or they will be sad the rest of the day," he said, walking over toward the greeters. Megan hesitated and then followed after him and shook their hands.

Sally took this all in with wonderment. Cassie wasn't kidding about them being friendly here, she thought. Then it really got confusing. Next she was introduced to Lucy, and then Cassie dragged her over to meet her friend's parents. Before she could absorb all that she was swooped into the sanctuary and into a pew just as the minister was welcoming everyone to the service. Then everyone was standing up and shaking hands or hugging each other. *How will I ever remember all of those names?* she wondered.

She remained unfocused through the first hymn, comparing this to her experience at church as a child. They would always get there early, go directly to their pew, and sit quietly until the service started. When the service ended, they would all wait in line to file past the minister, making polite small talk until it was their turn to shake his hand. Sally had actually seen some people clapping time during the hymn. She couldn't imagine that happening in her parents' church.

The children's minister invited the children through the fifth grade to come to the front for the children's moment. Don motioned for Megan to go, but she clung to her mother's arm. Cassie reached across two people, took Megan's hand, and whispered something to her. Megan reluctantly followed Cassie down to the front. When they were dismissed to go to children's church, Cassie marched Megan out with the others, giving her no chance to protest. *Who's child is that?* thought Sally, shaking her head.

After the service, Robby ushered his mother out to a gathering area where there were tables of coffee, juices, and several kinds of bagels. People were everywhere, talking in small groups, catching up on one another's lives. Robby saw some friends and abandoned her just as Cassie and Megan showed up.

"Mommy, that was fun. Can we come back next week?" asked Megan excitedly.

"Yes" was all Sally could think of to say.

"We'll see you after Sunday school," said Cassie, and they took off again before Sally could protest.

Then just as suddenly, Lucy was standing beside her with a woman about her age. "Sally, I'd like you to meet Jenny. If you are interested in going to Sunday school, Jenny is in a class with people around your age."

Sally just stood there; she had no idea what she was getting in to. "You don't have to come; just know that you are welcome." Jenny smiled, noticing Sally's indecision.

What am I going to do? Just stand here looking lost until my kids get out of their classes? "Thank you. I think I'll join you." Sally smiled back, wondering where the words came from.

As the class broke up, Cassie and Megan suddenly materialized again. "Did you like it, Mommy?" asked Megan.

"Yes, I did. It was very interesting," Sally answered. "Did you like your class?"

"I didn't know any of the answers," Megan said sourly. "But I liked the stories. And I knew three other people in the class," she added, brightening.

"So you still want to come back next week?"

"Yes," Megan said emphatically. "Do you?"

"Yes, I think I do," her mother answered. "How do we find Robby?"

"He's back in the gym shooting baskets," said Cassie. "I'll show you. We can go out that way."

On the drive home, listening to her children share what went on in their classes with each other, Sally once again compared her own childhood recollection of church with what she had just experienced. She didn't know if her parents' church even had Sunday school. If they did, they never went. And she couldn't remember ever looking forward to coming back the next week like her kids were. How was she ever going to relate all this to Jack?

It was well after the kids went to bed that Sally finally told Jack about her experience at church. She had waited, hoping he would ask her about it, but it was obvious he wasn't going to. After church she had changed clothes, eaten a quick lunch, and hurried off to work without having a chance to say much to him. She heard the girls telling him about their classes and noticed that he was just listening and not asking any questions. She thought she would probably get the same treatment.

"You haven't asked me what I thought about the whole church thing," she started.

"I figured you'd tell me if you wanted to."

"You aren't curious?"

"The kids seemed to enjoy it."

"You didn't answer my question." Sally would not be denied.

Jack sighed. "I know you're going to tell me how friendly everyone was and how nice they are to my kids and that I should not judge this church by what happened to me. But I can't do that. To me, church is a place to go to feel guilty. I don't want to feel guilty."

"You're right; I am going to tell you those things, but it was much more than that."

Sally waited for Jack to ask her, "Like what?" But he didn't. So she told him anyway. She was determined that he was going to hear it.

"Those people weren't there just because it was Sunday and that's what you're supposed to do. They were there because they wanted to be there. They were happy to be there. It wasn't stiff and cold like I remember it. I went to a Sunday school class with people mostly our age. They shared problems with each other and then found Bible verses to help deal with them. Almost everyone had something to say."

"What did you say?"

"I was introduced, and I said a little bit about my family. I didn't take part in the discussion."

"Why not?"

"I didn't feel comfortable. I just listened to people trying to help each other with their problems. And I didn't notice anyone feeling guilty."

"Maybe you could go back next week and tell them that your husband is unemployed and you're working two jobs and we don't have any health insurance and we expect any day now to get a foreclosure notice on our home. Maybe they could solve those problems," Jack said bitterly.

"I enjoyed going there today, Jack, and I'm not going to let you spoil it for me because you feel guilty about not having a job. Nobody's blaming you for being out of work except you. I'm going again next week to see if it's always that way. Maybe you should go and ask if anyone has any ideas about how you can make up with your kids for being rude to their friend. You still haven't done that. Ignoring it won't make it go away."

Jack knew he deserved the rebuke. He had gone out of his way to be solicitous to his children, to the point of not disciplining them when he should have, but he had not apologized to them. He knew he had to do it, and he knew he had to start with Robby. *Tomorrow I'm just going to do it*, he told himself.

CHAPTER 11

Jack's plans changed when he opened the mail on Monday. There was a foreclosure notice from the bank, something he had been dreading for weeks. They had scraped together enough money to make the payment just before the end of the grace period in November. In December and January they were late and had to pay a penalty. That was when they got their first warning notice. "Nothing will happen unless you actually start missing payments. The letter was to merely alert you that you need to pay close attention to the due dates so your account doesn't become delinquent," the unfriendly woman at the bank had said when he called.

In February they simply didn't have enough money to make the payment. Jack called the bank again, talked his way past the unhelpful woman he had talked to before, and was passed on to an assistant manager who wasn't any better. Jack asked him if they could pay just the interest due for the month.

"You can make an application for an interest-only loan," said the voice.

"How much would that cost me?" asked Jack, knowing that whatever it was, he didn't have it.

"That would depend." The man sounded bored.

"On what?"

"A number of things." He sighed. "The current value of your house compared to the balance of your mortgage, your employment status, your credit rating, to mention a few. The interest rate would depend largely on your ability to pay."

"I need to know how much it will cost me to convert my loan, what the new interest rate would be, and how much my payments would be." Jack's exasperation showed in his voice.

The man took all of the details he needed from Jack and said he would get back to him with estimates of those numbers. Jack did not appreciate his patronizing tone and wondered if he would call him back.

He didn't, but a few days later a friendly and helpful young man named Jeff did. Jeff explained the entire foreclosure process to Jack and told him that with all of the possible delays and any successful appeals, they might have another eight to ten months before they would have to get out of their house after the process was started.

"What if I could make another payment soon?" Jack asked. They almost had enough money to do that, but not enough to pay the accumulated penalties.

"Well, if you made a payment, it would complicate things for the bank and probably cause a delay," Jeff told him. "But if you were able to catch up altogether, including penalties, the whole process would be stopped."

Fat chance, unless I get a job, thought Jack. "What about the interest-only loan?" he asked.

Jeff didn't answer right away. "That doesn't look too promising," he said finally. "First of all, the loan application fee is two hundred dollars and has to be paid up front. The rest of the closing costs can be added to the amount of the loan." Jeff paused. "The bad part is that because of your credit score, the interest rate would be unusually high and the payments wouldn't be much less than they are now."

Jack sighed and slumped his shoulders. "So what are you telling me?"

"I really doubt that your application would be accepted, even at the high interest rate. At least until you get steady employment," Jeff said honestly.

That was over two months ago, and they hadn't made a payment since. They had almost made it in March, but a two hundred-dollar car repair got in the way. They thought about letting Sally drive the truck but decided that it was too risky to drive it that much without insurance. So far they had been lucky with Jack just driving it when he could find work. Now they were about to miss their May payment unless a job opportunity dropped out of the sky in the next few days. Jack had just started to read over the foreclosure notice again when Robby came in the door.

After another long discussion with Jay after the youth program on Sunday, Robby had decided to talk to his dad about the work mission. He would come home directly after school on Monday and get it over with before his sisters showed up. He really wanted to go. Jay had warned him not to be confrontational but to explain to his dad how important it was to him. He prayed about it before he went to sleep that night. He had been doing more and more of that lately.

Now he was almost home, feeling not at all confident. He had rehearsed his speech all day but knew when the time came he would mess it up. He looked up to the sky, said, "Help me to be cool," and went in the door. His dad was sitting at the kitchen table, his chin resting in one hand, staring at a letter he was holding in the other.

"Hi, Dad," said Robby, hoping his voice didn't betray his nervousness. The expression on his dad's face was something Robby had never seen before.

"What's wrong?" Jack just looked at him, as though he didn't see him "Dad?"

Jack collected himself and said in a hollow voice, "Nothing. How was school?"

"Something happened. Tell me!"

Jack dropped the letter and buried his face in his hands. Robby picked it up and started to read it. "They're going to take our house," Jack said quietly, his voice muffled by his hands.

"When?" was all Robby could think of to say, realizing that the nightmare was finally coming true. What would happen to them?

Jack looked up at him, trying to remember what Jeff had told him. "I'm not sure. Probably six months. I don't know."

"You'll have a job by then. More people are going back to work all the time."

"It's so slow. None of the guys I worked with have found anything."

"You can't give up," said Robby.

"I don't know what else I can do," Jack said softly, putting his head back in his hands.

"Dad, you've tried so hard for so long; you can't quit now!" Robby was shouting. "What about all that stuff you've always told me about the game of baseball being like the game of life? If I was in a slump, I had to keep trying. Never give up; it'll get better. What about all that stuff? Besides I know a way we can…" Robby stopped himself from saying what Don had said about the church helping them out with money. Upset with himself for doing what he had been determined not to do, he turned and headed back to his room.

Jack sat there trying to sort out what had just happened. He rolled Robby's words over in his mind. Of course he had said those things. *That's what you say to kids. And you expect them to believe it. But do I believe it? If Robby would have kept going he probably would have said that I'm about ready to take a called third strike. Maybe I am.*

Jack picked up the foreclosure notice again. He recalled some of the things his father had said to him. Nothing positive. If something bad happened to you, God was punishing you for something you did wrong. It was always your own fault. Sooner or later you were going to pay for your sins. *Is this it? Was my dad right?* Is that what he would hear if he asked his dad for a small loan to get them through this? He had thought about it but never seriously. Sally had mentioned it once. Is that what Robby meant when he stopped talking? *I know he's worried. What can I say to reassure him?* Jack slowly pushed himself away from the table and went back to talk to his son.

Robby flopped facedown on his bed, frightened about what he had just learned, angry with himself for his outburst, and surprised that his dad hadn't lashed back at him. Plus, he knew for sure he wouldn't get to go on the work mission. He found himself bouncing from one of those problems to the other, unable to concentrate on any one of them. But he came back most often to wondering why his accusing words hadn't led to an ugly exchange between him and his father. Was his dad so discouraged that he didn't have any fight left in him? Why couldn't he talk to his dad like he did Don and Jay? Finally he just lay there trying to block all thoughts from his mind. Then he heard his door opening. He rolled over and saw his dad in the doorway.

"I'm not going to quit, Robby," his father said. "I don't want you to worry about that. We're going to get through this."

"I'm sorry I said those things," blurted Robby.

"Sometimes you need to hear things you don't want to. I think maybe I needed that scolding."

Robby bit at his lower lip, fighting back tears.

Jack walked over and sat on the end of the bed. "The man at the bank said if we could catch up before they actually foreclosed, we could keep our house. You were right; I can get a job before that happens, and things will work out."

"How much would it be?" Robby was wondering if Don could get enough.

"Well, we're almost four months behind, and our payments are a little over six hundred dollars a month, so with the penalties, it's over twenty-eight hundred dollars right now."

Robby's heart sank. He thought Don was probably talking about a few hundred dollars. "What if you just pay part of it?"

"The man said that would probably delay it, and it was a good idea to do it. Why?"

Robby hesitated. "Can I tell you something and you won't get mad?"

"Are you thinking about robbing a bank?" Jack smiled.

"No!" he exclaimed much too quickly, causing Jack to get a puzzled look on his face.

"What, then?"

Robby sat up in his bed, closed his eyes, and exhaled, not sure how to start. *Just say it,* he told himself. "Don says the people at the church can help us out." He waited for the explosion.

Jack's jaw muscles tensed. "You know how I feel about charity," he said evenly.

"I told Don that. He said we could pay it back when we got back on our feet."

"A loan?"

"No. It's up to you. Whenever you feel like you can do it, you just give a gift to the church. If you want to. You don't have to. And it doesn't matter how much it is." Robby wasn't sure he was explaining it very well.

"That church is just going to hand us money—someone they don't know—and we don't have to pay it back unless we want to? Do you really believe that?" Jack didn't. He wondered if Robby had his facts straight.

"No, Dad. It's not the church; it's the people." Robby struggled to get his words in the right order. He knew he was going to talk too fast and leave things out. But he had to do it; his dad was actually listening to him. "Okay, they spread the word that someone needs help, and they're going to collect money for them. There's this guy who collects the money. People give him money; he puts it in an envelope, never looks at it, never counts it; and they give it to the people who need it. Don said they don't do it very often, but he would put the request out if we would accept the money."

Jack sat there, digesting all that. *A few hundred dollars would let us make the May payment. But the whole world would know about it.* "So everybody knows who the money is for."

"No. They don't tell who it is. Only Don knows. And they only give cash, so we don't know who they are. The guy who collects the money gives it to Don, and he gives it to us." *I left that part out,* Robby scolded himself.

Robby waited, watching Jack alternating between clenching and unclenching his hands and cracking his knuckles. If his dad was really considering it, he didn't want to interrupt him. He lay back down on the bed and breathed a small prayer of thanks for at least getting this far. And without an argument.

"I don't know, Robby. That's a lot to think about. I'm not sure I could do it. It would be hard for me," Jack said in slow, halting sentences, staring at his hands. "I need to talk to your mother," he added, turning and giving Robby a small, sad smile. "I have to tell her about the notice."

Robby closed his eyes. *Okay, I think I know what Mom will say. But what about the work mission? Is it safe to bring that up now?*

"Not good enough?" he heard his father saying.

"Yeah! Sure." Robby sat back up. "I was just thinking about something else."

"There's more?"

"Sort of."

Jack waited.

"Dad, they're going on this work mission, and I want to go."

The words weren't out of his mouth when they heard the kitchen door crash open, followed by the sounds of girls all talking at once and backpacks being dumped on the floor. His sisters were home. "Where is everyone?" they heard Cassie shout. Robby slumped back down on the bed and put his hands over his face.

"Oh, there you are," said Cassie, bursting into the room. "What's wrong," she asked, looking at Robby.

"Nothing." Jack smiled. "Robby was just whining about a homework assignment and not getting the sympathy he was looking for. How many of you are there?" he asked, seeing more girls behind her.

"Oh, this is Emily, Kiana and Lindsi, friends from church. They just came over to hang out for a while."

"Well, hang away," said Jack.

He shook their hands and hugged his daughters. "I'd better get started on dinner; your mom's only working till six tonight." He turned back to Robby and said, "We'll talk about your problem later this evening."

Cassie gave Robby a "what's with him look," and he gave her an "I don't know" shrug back.

The girls left, and Robby stayed on his bed, trying to figure out his dad. He had just acted like his old self. Cassie had noticed it too. They talked to each other without getting mad. His dad had thought that Robby was scolding him; he chuckled to himself. *And he made up that story about me having homework problems. Does this prayer thing really work?* His feeling of dread about talking to his dad about the work mission was gone. He was almost sure he would get to go.

Then he thought about the quarters. *Why can't I forget about that?* But he knew he had to face it. He knew it wouldn't go away. *Maybe if things stay good with Dad for a while, I'll get a chance to tell him and Mom,* he decided. *But I don't envy him having to tell Mom about the house.*

CHAPTER 12

While he was making dinner and during the meal, Jack could feel all of his anxieties coming back. He knew his brief connection with his son had wiped them away temporarily, but now he had to tell Sally about the letter. She seemed more tired than usual. By the time the meal was over, Jack was overwhelmed by a feeling of dread. When Robby got up from the table, he gave his father a look of understanding that felt like a pat on the back.

Jack stalled around in the kitchen cleaning up after the meal, putting off the inevitable. He didn't know whether to tell Sally or just hand her the letter. He knew that losing the house was her biggest fear, with one of the kids getting sick close behind. What would she think about the offer of money from the church? He remembered his outburst at Christmas when she signed up for the food bank. He still regretted that even though she understood and clearly had forgiven him. Sally was doing what she could to take care of her family, and he had been wrong for making her cancel it. Would she be afraid to say what she thought now? Maybe not, because he was the one bringing it up.

But how did he feel? Would he be backing down on his principles because he was desperate, or was he letting his pride stand in the way in the first place, like he had at Christmas? And then there was the work mission thing that Robby had thrown at him just as the girls were coming home. Where were they going? For how long? Was it going to cost money? Of course. He had told Robby he would talk to him about it, but first things first.

Jack gave the kitchen counter one last wipe down and went into the living room right at the end of *Jeopardy!* He scooted the kids off to do their homework and appreciated that Robby took the lead by going right away without a whimper.

"Did you decide to wash down the walls and scrub the floor tonight?" Sally said teasingly, referring to his lengthy stay in the kitchen.

"Somebody had to do it," he answered lamely, trying unsuccessfully to smile.

"What's wrong?"

Jack pursed his lips and tried to think of a way to put it off. "I had a good talk with Robby this afternoon."

"He told me some of it. What's wrong?"

I can't hide anything from her, he thought to himself. Sally waited. "We got a foreclosure notice in the mail today," he told her simply, his voice cracking slightly.

Sally set her tea mug down and drummed her fingers beside it on the end table. "What exactly does that mean?" Sally already knew the answer; they had talked about it several times.

"What it means is the bank is going to take our house in about six months if we don't catch up on our payments."

"How close are we to making this month's payment?"

"Two hundred and fifty bucks, give or take," Jack answered, not sure where she was going.

"What else can we sell?"

"Sally, if we sold everything we have, it wouldn't keep it from happening." His frustration was obvious.

"We have to do everything we can to delay this until you get a job. This is our home," Sally shot back with more emotion than he expected. He could tell she was close to tears.

They sat there looking at each other across the room, neither of them saying anything. Finally Jack got up and sat by Sally on the couch. He put his arm around her, pulled her close to him, and kissed her on the forehead. "We'll find a way," he said softly, wiping the wetness from her face. "Robby came up with an idea."

"What!" she pushed away and looked up at him. "You told him?"

"He walked in just after I opened the letter. He knew something was wrong. I couldn't lie to him."

"What did he say?"

"He pretty much freaked out."

"Describe that to me."

"Well,"—Jack chuckled—"he gave me a lecture about not giving up. Didn't pull any punches. Pretty much took me to the woodshed."

"Then what happened?" Sally wasn't sure she wanted to know.

"He stomped off to his room."

"You didn't say anything back?"

"Nothing to say. He was right. He's not a kid anymore."

"I'm afraid he's had to grow up too fast," Sally said sadly.

"I think it bothers Cassie a lot too."

"What about telling the girls?"

"I don't know. I'm not ready for that yet." *How would I explain it to them?* Jack wondered.

"So what was Robby's idea? You said he stomped off."

"His friend Don told him that the church would collect money to help us out." Sally just looked at him, her face unreadable. "Nobody would know who we are, and we could pay it back when things got back to normal."

"You would do that?" Sally asked after a long silence.

"I don't know. I wanted to know what you think."

Sally thought about it. "I don't know either. I'm not sure I understand it." Her answer surprised him. He thought she would just say do it.

"According to Robby, they would tell the people that there was a family that needed money and anyone interested in helping them could give an anonymous gift. They have a man who collects it, and he would give it to Don. All of the money is in envelopes, nobody sees it, nobody counts it, and Don would hand it over to us. He would be the only person who knows who we are."

"It sounds good if it works that way. How would they know if we paid it back?" Sally sounded skeptical.

"I guess they wouldn't unless we sent a thank-you note along with it." Jack was puzzled by Sally's reaction.

They both fell silent again. Sally picked up her mug and took a sip of tea long since gone cold. "Jack, I think I would be uncomfortable if people knew we were given money like that."

"You signed up for the food bank."

"I know, but that was different. These would be people I know; people I probably sit in Sunday school class with."

"So you would be embarrassed?"

Sally took another sip of tea and made a face. Jack took the cup from her and headed toward the microwave. "You could have taken the hint the first time." She laughed as he disappeared into the kitchen.

Jack brought back the now hot tea and waited for her answer. "I think I would be. And what about the kids? Would they get teased about it?"

Jack didn't say anything. "I really like the people I've met at church," Sally started again. "I think I'm making some friends. And I'm seeing the whole Jesus and God thing in a whole new light. It's starting to make sense to me. And I like what I'm finding out. Maybe all the trouble we're having is so we can get connected to God." Sally watched Jack's face, wondering if she'd gone too far.

"You mean like this is the punishment for everything we've ever done wrong," Jack said sourly.

"No, I mean this could be God's way of forcing us to let him help us through the people of the church. We sure weren't going to ask him."

Where did she get an idea like that? Jack wondered. This was not the first time she had brought up God in their conversations. Jack had always ignored the comments or changed the subject. He could see that the church was having an effect on her. But not in a bad way. *If it works for her and the kids, fine. If they're happy, I'm happy.*

"So are you rejecting the money offer?" Jack asked her.

Sally sighed, giving up on the God angle for the time being. "I'm unsure," she answered. "I think you should talk to Don about it and make sure we understand all the details."

"I doubt that he would give me the time of day," said Jack, recalling his encounter with Don back in February.

"He's not angry with you, Jack. He told Robby that he understands what you're going through and was not offended. He was very friendly to me at church."

"You're not the one who attacked him," he protested. Sally gave him the look. "Okay. I'll think about it," he said, knowing there was no use arguing.

"Good," she said, giving him her "I win again" smile.

"What do you know about this work mission Robby wants to go on?" Jack asked, changing the subject.

"Not much. They talked about it in church. They're raising money to go to Wisconsin to rebuild flooded-out homes. I'm not sure when— in June, I guess. Did he say something to you?"

"Yes, just when the girls came home, so we didn't get to talk about it. I told him we would talk later. I guess I better go do it," Jack said, getting up.

"I'll go check on the girls," said Sally.

Robby was sprawled out on his bed, plugged into his iPod, when Jack walked into his room. He got it for his twelfth birthday, before his dad was laid off. Jack sat down on the desk chair while Robby untangled himself from all the wires.

"Well, did you get your homework problem solved?" Jack asked, with a smile.

Robby laughed. "Turned out not to be so bad. What about you? How'd that go?"

"You're mother was upset, of course, but it wasn't unexpected. We just didn't know when. I know you're concerned, but try not to worry about it." Robby just looked at him. "That was a dumb thing to say. Of course you're going to worry about it. How about, trust us that we'll get us all through it?"

"I'll try." Robby sighed.

"Now tell me about this work mission business."

"Okay, every year Jay takes the kids from the youth program somewhere to do volunteer work. This year they're going to Wisconsin to work on flooded houses. Right now about twenty kids and eight adults are going. We leave on Saturday morning and come back the following Sunday."

Jack digested all that information. "You didn't mention anything about cost."

Robby bit his lip. "Jay said it's already paid for."

"Explain that." Jack was frowning. *More charity?*

"Well, first of all, they have a lot of fundraisers that pay for a lot of the trip for everyone. But if somebody can't pay for the rest, there's a scholarship fund that pays for them. Anyone who wants to go gets to go. Jay said if the church found out that someone got left out because of money, he would be in for a public flogging."

Jack fiddled with a pencil from Robby's desk. "I really want to go, Dad," Robby said after a while.

"That's a long time to be gone. You've never been away from home before."

Robby rolled his eyes. "I'm fourteen years old, Dad," he said with just a trace of attitude.

Jack tapped the pencil against the palm of his hand. *So much for that argument,* he thought. *They want to help pay for my mortgage. They want to pay my kid's way on this trip. What are they going to want from me? I'm not comfortable with this. But it's important to Robby. How can I tell him no?* "Let me think about it" was all he could think of to say.

Robby couldn't sleep; his mind was in turmoil. He had actually shouted at his dad, and his dad hadn't shouted back. His dad had listened to him as if what he said mattered. And he hadn't said no to the work mission. Would he let him go? Would he accept the help Don offered? Robby had a lot of stuff to tell Jay and Don.

CHAPTER 13

"I still can't believe it," said Robby while picking at the remnants of his third taco. Robby had just finished telling Don the details of his conversations with his father on Monday.

"You actually said those things to him?" Don asked, sipping on a Diet Pepsi.

"Yes."

"And he didn't get mad?"

"I stopped myself from saying something about money from the church and went right to my room. He didn't say anything. I thought I'd really messed up," Robby answered.

Robby waited while Don processed all that he had told him. "Here's what I think," Don said finally. "I think you walked in on your dad when he was still reeling from that letter, and your outburst caught him off guard. But not so much that he didn't hear the words that you said. I think hearing from you that you knew how hard he was trying meant a lot to him. I think not only the words that you spoke but also the passion, and maybe a little bit of fear in your voice, went straight to his heart. What you said and how you said it made him realize that he had your support and gave him the lift he needed. And I think what he said to you about needing a scolding was his way of saying thank you."

Robby slurped up the last of his drink and stirred the remaining ice with the straw, thinking about what Don had just said. It seemed as though he had done the wrong thing and it had turned out all right. He had vowed not to raise his voice, and it was the first thing he did. It just didn't make sense.

"Maybe God is using you to get connected to your dad," said Don, interrupting his thoughts.

"What do you mean?"

"I told you in our first conversation that maybe God had you steal those quarters so our church could help your family. Maybe his bigger plan is to use all this as a way to get through to your dad. Your dad has completely shut him out. God hasn't been a part of your family's life at all. But he is now, except for your dad, and he wants him too."

"He's not making much progress," said Robby.

"I think what happened on Monday was progress."

"How?" Robby didn't see it.

"If you would have said anything to your dad before Monday about either the work mission or accepting money from the church he would probably dismissed it with no discussion. Now he's apparently considering both."

"You think God made me say what I did?"

"It wouldn't surprise me. You didn't intend to do it, and now you and your dad are communicating." Don smiled.

Robby didn't say anything. "Have you talked to him about any of that since?" Don asked.

"Nope. My mom told him to call you about the money and get more details, and he said he'd think about it."

"It would take us a while to get the money collected. We probably couldn't get it done in time to make the mortgage payment before they tacked on another penalty." Don figured it would take three weeks to make it happen. "I can't go ahead unless he calls me and agrees to it."

They emptied their trays into the trash bin and went out to Don's van to go get Cassie.

"My mom's not sure about it either. She's afraid people will find out and she will be embarrassed."

"How could anyone possibly figure it out? Did you tell her how we'd do it?" Don had thought that Sally would be all for it.

"I told them both just what you told me. Nobody would know but you."

"Did she feel that way about the work mission?" Don asked.

"That didn't seem to bother her."

"And you feel good about your dad letting you go?"

Robby frowned and thought how to answer that. "I thought he was going to say I could go right then, but he just said he would think about it. And I haven't brought it up again."

"I hope you get to go," said Don as they walked into the church.

"I think I at least have a chance," said Robby honestly.

They were just starting down the hall to the gym when someone called out to Don from behind them. They turned to see the minister coming from the narthex. "Hi, Scot," said Don. "What's up?"

"I need to talk to you if you have a minute. Hi, Robby."

"Hi," Robby said back.

"Sure," said Don. "We're just coming to pick up Cassie. You go get her and meet me back here," he said, turning to Robby. "No hurry if you need to talk to Jay," he added, knowing Robby would want to tell Jay about what went on with his father.

"I see that his family's coming almost every Sunday now," said Scot.

"Except the dad."

"What's his story?"

"Robby has told me bits and pieces, but I'm not sure I'm getting the whole story. Apparently his parents were members of a very fundamentalist church that only talked about an angry, punishing God and left out the forgiveness and grace part. Robby said he's only seen his grandparents a few times in his life, and it was always uncomfortable. His father evidently had a very unhappy childhood. He had a job lined up to go to when he graduated from high school and moved out the next day."

"Have you met him?" Scot asked.

"Oh, yeah. He will have nothing to do with the church," said Don sourly.

"How'd that go?" Scot smiled, sensing an interesting story.

"The little girl, Megan, asked me if she could take the *Beatrice's Goat* book to school, so I took it to their house. I also took some pictures of our trip to Honduras, and when he saw them, he accused me of telling his kids that even though they were poor they were better off than other kids around the world."

"He said that to you?" Scot looked skeptical. "In front of the kids?"

"He did."

"Are they poor?"

"Well, Jack hasn't worked for almost a year, and they're really struggling to make mortgage payments. He's been able to find odd jobs but not often enough. Sally works two part-time jobs. He's under a lot of stress. I think his self-esteem is pretty low and he doesn't want some old church guy influencing his kids. Given his background and the situation, his reaction was not surprising." Don was on the brink of telling Scot about the foreclosure notice.

Scot thought about that. "You weren't offended?"

Don chuckled. "I spent a lot of time in construction trailers arguing with unreasonable contractors. I didn't tell Jack, but compared to them, he's a lightweight. My concern was for the kids. I felt really bad for them."

Don waited for a response. "Do you think he's still mad at his parents?" Scot asked after a while.

"What do you mean?"

"Could he still be carrying around a lot of anger because of his treatment as a child, and now his family's involvement with the church has brought it to the surface? Maybe he's never forgiven them. Maybe he doesn't know how. Maybe he doesn't know he needs to. For him."

"I'll have to think about that," said Don, already doing so.

"While you're doing that, think about this. I was looking for you because I thought you might be able to help me solve a problem, and it seems that God may have handed us the solution on a silver platter."

"Well, that's clear as mud," said Don, having no clue what Scot was talking about.

"It will be." Scot smiled. "I got a phone call from Alice Marshall this afternoon asking me if I knew of anyone who was out of work and might be interested in painting her house. She would rather pay someone who was out of a job than hire a contractor. Is your sight improving?"

"Rapidly."

"Plus, you will be talking to Jack under much more favorable circumstances, and maybe you will get an opportunity to help him with his eyesight," Scot added smugly.

Before Don could think of a clever response, Robby and Cassie came walking down the hall. "Sorry we took so long. I was talking to Jay," Robby apologized.

"Forever." Cassie rolled her eyes.

"Your timing is perfect," said Don. "Hi, Cassie."

"Hi," said Cassie, giving him a hug.

"Hello, Cassie," said Scot.

"Hi, Pastor Scot," she said, rewarding him with a hug also.

"I have to get these two home," Don said to Scot. "I'll get started on that tomorrow."

"Let me know."

CHAPTER 14

The next morning Don was trying to decide how to approach Jack about the painting job. He knew Jack harbored deep feelings against the church, but was he softening? His family was getting comfortably connected to the church; that must be having some effect on him, or at least be making him wonder. And then there was the matter of Alice herself. She was a character in her own right—a spinster who didn't mince words, rumored to have a lot of money squirreled away. But she was a generous giver to the church and generally liked by everyone. He was trying to picture her and Jack getting along.

He decided he needed to know more details about what she wanted, so he called Scot.

"She told me she has been putting it off for a couple of years, so there could be a lot of scraping and crack filling. I think it's a pretty old house," Scot told him.

"It is old," said Don, "but I think it's probably in fairly good shape. I'm surprised she's let something like this go; it's not like her. I'll just take Jack over there—if he'll go—and we'll see what there is to it."

"I'll call her and tell her to expect you. When do you think you'll go?"

"I'll go see Jack right after lunch, so sometime right after that."

Jack was washing his truck, wondering if he was doing the right thing. He had decided to clean it up and put a "for sale" sign on it. Most of the small jobs he had been doing were because friends he had worked with called him to help them. So, he reasoned, most of the time he could probably get a ride with them. They had done that sometimes anyway. There would be times when he would have to take Sally to work, and that could get complicated. The kids would be getting out of school soon, so they wouldn't need to be hauled around as much.

The biggest problem with it was he would have to take a lot less than it was worth—or would have been worth a year ago. A five-year-old truck with barely forty thousand miles on it and well taken care of would be a good buy for someone. But buyers today, if there were any, knew that anyone selling a truck like that was doing it because they had to. He would at least test the waters; he didn't have to sell it. If he couldn't get enough to save his house he wouldn't do it.

Jack was spraying the last of the soap off the hood when Don pulled up and parked across the street. Jack glanced up. He didn't recognize the van, but he recognized the driver. It was a warm early May afternoon, and Don had the window down. *What is this?* Jack thought, tensing up. He remembered his promise to Sally that he would call Don, but he could never bring himself to do it. Jack could feel his animosity returning. He was not going to take money from this guy.

"Hello, Jack," said Don, as he crossed the street. "I don't know if you remember me."

"The church guy," said Jack, starting to wipe down his truck.

"I've never been called that before," Don responded lightly. "My name is Don." *This is not going to be fun*, he thought.

"I remember," said Jack, going right on wiping, not looking at Don. "Thanks for the offer, but we're not going to take your money."

Don waited to see if there would be more. There wasn't. Apparently he had been dismissed. For a fleeting second he thought about walking away. "That's not why I came," Don said evenly, walking to the other side of the truck so Jack couldn't turn his back to him.

Jack stopped and looked at Don. "Am I going to get a lecture about how I should go to church with my family?"

"Would you listen?"

Jack bent down and wiped the side of the truck, ignoring the question. Don waited until Jack straightened back up.

"The minister at my church told me that an elderly member of our congregation was looking for someone to paint her house and wondered if I knew of anybody who might be interested."

Jack just looked at him. *I am such an idiot*, he berated himself. *That's twice I've misjudged him.* "Look, I'm sorry..."

Don put up his hands. "Are you interested?" he interrupted.

"Why don't you just tell me to stuff it and walk away?"

"I'm close. Are you interested?"

Jack leaned against his truck with his head on his arms. "Yes," he said, "I am."

"Finish wiping down your truck, and we'll go look at the job."

While Jack finished the truck, Don rolled up the hose and then waited while Jack locked up the house.

"Where is it?" Jack asked.

"Over on the west side, about ten minutes from here. On Jackson just off of Broadway," Don answered, wondering at the question.

"How long do you think it will take?"

"I don't know. Depends on how many questions you have and how talkative Alice is. You have to be somewhere?"

Jack looked at his watch. Almost two o'clock. "No, but I have to get to the store and then have dinner ready for Sally so she can get to work by six. She's sleeping right now. The store's sort of over that way, so we better drive separately. I'll follow you."

Or you don't want to be trapped in a car with me, thought Don.

Don pulled into Alice's driveway, but Jack parked on the street. Jack leaned on the fender of his truck with his arms folded, looking at the house. It was a big two-story with a porch all the way across the front and two dormers sticking out of the second floor. Don started walking toward Jack when the front door opened.

"Well, are you coming in?" said a voice from behind the screen door.

"Oh, hi, Alice," said Don, looking her way. "I think we'll just look around first to see what we're dealing with."

"Suit yourself," she said and closed the door.

Don continued walking over to Jack. "What are you thinking?" he asked.

"That you must think I'm a big jerk."

Don smiled. "I would if I didn't know your family. They wouldn't be the way they are if you were really a jerk—all the time."

"Just part of the time's okay?" Jack almost allowed himself to smile.

"Well, it's not that you don't have plenty of reasons to be upset, but you've got to stop fighting whatever you're fighting. You're punishing your family while you're punishing yourself." Jack looked at him, not comprehending.

"I have a theory," said Don. "Want to hear it?"

Jack bit at his lower lip, thinking.

That must be where Robby gets that from, thought Don.

"Go ahead," said Jack finally.

"Actually, it's my pastor's theory. He asked me if I knew why you didn't come to church with your family, and I told him what I know about it from Robby." Jack started to say something then inhaled and stopped himself. Don knew he was operating close to a large nerve. "Scot wonders if all this stress has caused some anger you have suppressed toward your parents to work its way to the surface without you realizing it. That your anger isn't really toward the church but toward your parents, and you resent sharing your family with the church. I also told him you were out of work, and that's when he told me about this job."

Jack pushed himself away from the truck and walked over to the middle of the front yard, looking up at the house. *Time to shut up*, thought Don. *At least he didn't hit me.*

After a long while, Jack spoke. "I hated church when I was a kid and hated my parents for making me go. I hated the way I was treated because of the church. I think I even hated myself most of the time." Don waited, wondering if there was more. Jack turned to face him. "It wasn't like that for you, was it?"

"When I was a kid, we went to about five different churches because of moving around, and it was never like that—not even close," said Don. "And in all the different places my wife and I have ended up around the country, we've never encountered an unfriendly church of any size or variety. I'm not disputing your word, but my experience has been the exact opposite of yours."

Jack walked closer to the house. "Guess I was just lucky," he threw back over his shoulder.

"I know there's a lot more to this than I've heard from Robby and from what I just heard from you. You need to find a way to put it behind you. If you ever want to get a different perspective on the whole church thing, we can sit down and talk. Or talk to Pastor Scot—or both of us. I can give you a whole list of people."

The front door opened again. "Doesn't seem like you've done much looking," said Alice.

"Alice, forgive us." Don smiled. "We have been standing out here solving the world's problems—and failing miserably. We'll do it this time, I promise."

"I'll be here," she said and disappeared again.

They spent the next half hour working their way around the house, looking for anything unusual and figuring out what kind of equipment Jack would need. "Does she have any ladders?" asked Jack, looking toward the garage at the back of the lot.

"Doesn't matter; we've got all kinds of ladders in the garage at church. And scaffolding too. You might want to use a scaffold on those dormers," said Don.

Jack just looked at him. "What?" asked Don.

"You're not going to quit until you get me to take something from that church, are you?"

"Nope," said Don. "Let's go see Alice."

Don introduced them, and Alice offered them seats in the living room. "Well, do you want the job?" she said without preamble.

Taken off guard, Jack looked at Don. "Does he get to know how much it pays?" Don asked her.

"I got three prices. They all gave me a price for the paint and a price for labor. The lowest labor price was thirty-two hundred fifty dollars. Will you do it for that?"

Jack was stunned. At the most he thought he could get two thousand dollars. He took a deep breath and exhaled. "Sounds fair to me," was all he could think of to say.

"When will you start?" asked Alice.

Jack hesitated. "Do you have the paint?"

"It's on order; you can pick it up."

"Are you in a big hurry to have this done?" Jack asked uneasily.

"You got another job?"

"Most of the jobs I've been able to get have just popped up at the last minute, and I was wondering, if that happened, could I take time off to do it? Most of them have been just a day or day and a half." *She'll never go for that*, thought Jack, glancing at Don. He was looking much amused by this conversation. *Why doesn't he say something?*

Alice thought about that. "It would seem foolish not to, wouldn't it?"

"Thank you," said Jack, relieved.

"How bad is your trouble?" Alice asked him.

"What do you mean?" he asked, not sure what she meant.

"Well, you're not working, and you got bills to pay. Are you all caught up?"

"No," said Jack, wondering where she was going.

"How much do you need to catch up?"

She's going to pay me in advance, Jack realized. "Two hundred fifty-two dollars and thirty-two cents would let me pay my mortgage on time." He hadn't intended to say that and wanted to retract his words.

Before Jack could think of a way out of it, Alice walked over and got her checkbook from the dining room table, sat down, and started to write a check. She stopped and looked at Jack. "They tell us on the TV not to pay contractors anything in advance." She gave a sidelong look at Don. "But I know where to go if you run off with my money." Then she finished writing the check.

Jack looked over at Don, who was leaning back in his chair, smiling, and enjoying the moment. Alice held out the check to him. He got up and took it from her. Jack was stunned speechless. Five hundred dollars! He just stood there, shaking his head, looking stupid.

"Not enough?" asked Alice, smiling for the first time.

Jack composed himself enough to say, "You can't know how much this will mean to my family."

"Glad I could help," said the still-smiling Alice.

"Alice, we'll be back tomorrow with ladders and scaffolding so Jack can get started. It'll probably be late morning before we get everything together. I noticed a lot of overgrown bushes around your garage and by the back fence. Maybe a couple of us will stay and get rid of that for you tomorrow," said Don, getting up and moving toward the door.

"Don't bother; I told that youth director boy to send me someone who wanted to earn money for the mission. I haven't seen them yet, though."

"I'll take care of that for you. In fact, I'll have someone over here tomorrow after school," said Don. "Better yet, I'll have Jack take care of it."

"Consider it done," said Jack without hesitation.

"Your boy?" Alice asked him.

"My boy." Jack grinned.

"I'd like to go to the bank first thing in the morning with this check and get this month's payment taken care of," said Jack as they walked out to their vehicles.

"No problem. I'll never get anyone over there to help us before nine anyway. Get your business taken care of first."

"You're getting people to help?"

"Yeah, we can't load that stuff by ourselves. Besides, it'll take more than one truck to take it over there." Seeing Jack's baffled look, Don added, with a grin, "That's the way we do. Get used to it."

Jack didn't know what to do. He couldn't wait to get home to tell his family; but it was after four, and he hadn't been to the store to buy groceries for dinner. And Sally had to be at work at six. There just wasn't enough time. Then his phone rang. It was Sally.

"Where are you?"

"I'm sorry; something came up. I'm on my way home."

"What about dinner; should I start something? It's four fifteen." Her voice sounded anxious.

"I know. I'll take care of it. Trust me. I love you." And he hung up.

He drove into a shopping plaza and parked between a pizza store and a chicken shack. He ordered a large pizza to go and then went next door and got a bucket of chicken wings and two orders of fries. The pizza wasn't ready, so he walked three doors down to a convenience store and picked up two two-liter bottles of soda and a half gallon of ice cream. When he drove in his driveway, it was five minutes before five.

"What is going on?" asked Sally, as Jack struggled through the door with more than he could carry.

"I brought dinner." He grinned, half dropping it on the counter.

"Pizza!" cried Cassie and Megan in unison.

"Wings," said Robby, reaching into the bucket.

"Set the table first," said Jack.

"You still haven't told us what's going on," said Sally, frowning at him. He gave her a kiss and said, "I got Robby a job."

They all stopped what they were doing and looked at him. "Finish setting the table, and I'll tell you about it."

After they were all seated and had some food, Jack started his story. "There's a woman from the church—Alice Marshall is her name—who needs some overgrown bushes around her garage and fence trimmed up and wants to give the job to someone going on that work mission, so I told her that Robby would do it."

Robby froze in mid-bite, the end of a pizza wedge sticking out of his mouth. "Does that mean he gets to go?" asked Cassie.

"What were you doing at her house?" asked Sally. Robby just sat there with a piece of unchewed pizza in his mouth.

"I started at the end of the story," confessed Jack. "I was washing the truck after lunch when your friend Don showed up. I was sure he was going to talk to me about taking money from the church, and I wasn't very pleasant to him."

"How not pleasant?" asked Sally.

"Very not pleasant. He almost walked away. But he didn't. He told me the minister asked him if he knew anyone who was out of work who would be interested in painting Alice's house, and that's why he was here."

"That's what Pastor Scot wanted to talk to Don about yesterday." Robby had rediscovered his voice. "I'll bet that's what they were talking about when we walked up," he said to Cassie. "Remember, Don said he would take care of something tomorrow?" Cassie nodded yes, not letting the question interrupt her eating. "Sorry, Dad," Robby apologized for interrupting.

"We went to her house to look at the job. We drove separately because I needed to go to the store afterward. Turns out it was a good thing I did. After we looked all around the house, we went in to talk to her, and the first thing she said was did I want the job. I didn't know what to say. Then Don asked her about the pay. She said she had gotten three prices and she would pay the lowest if I would do it for that." They all waited. "I don't know which part to tell next."

"Come on, Dad!" said Robby.

Jack was enjoying himself. "Three thousand two hundred fifty dollars," he said, ending the suspense.

That's more than the twenty-eight hundred we need to catch up on the loan, thought Robby. He breathed a small prayer of thanks.

"Does that mean … " Sally started, reaching for Jack's hand.

"Yes, it does," he said, giving her hand a squeeze. Tears welled up in Sally's eyes.

"What's wrong with Mommy?" asked Megan.

"She's happy," said Robby. *Maybe now she can stay that way.*

"Funny way to show it," said Cassie, feeling left out of what was going on.

"We have been very worried that we wouldn't have enough money to keep paying for our house and that the bank might take it from us," Jack explained. "Now we have enough so that can't happen."

"Thanks for telling me." Cassie scowled.

"We didn't want you to worry, honey," said Sally.

"Robby knew."

"Robby found out quite by accident," said Jack.

"Is that what you guys were talking about when we came home from school Monday?" asked Cassie, looking at her dad.

"Maybe," said Robby, feeling very much included, which got him another scowl from Cassie.

"Is there more? I have to go," said Sally, looking at her watch.

"I'll give you the long version later, but she gave me an advance so I can make this month's payment tomorrow."

"How much?" said Robby and Cassie in unison.

"Five hundred dollars."

"I like that lady!" squealed Megan, clapping her hands.

"I'm going to look a mess at work," said Sally, laughing through her tears. She wiped her eyes with the back of her hand, smudging mascara all over her face. Jack was fighting tears himself. He went over and wrapped his arms around her, found a clean spot on her face, and gave her a kiss.

She kissed him back and gave him another hug. "I really have to go," she said softly.

After Sally left, they finished their meal and Jack got out the ice cream. "Mommy didn't get any," said Megan sadly.

"I'll wait up for her and make sure she gets some," Jack assured her.

"Was the bank actually going to take our house?" asked Cassie.

Jack and Robby exchanged glances. Cassie waited. "Yes," said Jack finally. "We got a letter on Monday saying that they were starting the process. But it takes a long time for it to actually happen, so when I finish this job and get caught up on our payments, the process will be stopped. The advance Alice gave me will keep us from paying anymore penalties." Jack wasn't sure how much he had eased their fears.

"Can I help?" asked Robbie.

"With the painting? Not until you get those bushes trimmed up. There's a lot of work to it."

"Thanks for letting me go," said Robby.

"I think you knew you were going to get to go anyway." Jack smiled.

"I was pretty sure." Robby grinned.

"Can I help Robby so he can start helping you sooner?" asked Cassie. "I don't want any money."

"Don't think you would have any choice," said Jack.

"Why?"

"If I have Alice figured out at all, which I don't, she would pay you herself if she saw you helping."

"Then I'll just give it to Robby."

"No, you won't. Not if you earn it," protested Robby. "Jay said there is scholarship money that never gets used up, and I could get that if I didn't get enough on my own. But if you help me, then Dad could get done faster and he'd get paid sooner."

"Then I'll help—and with the painting too, if there's anything I can do," said Cassie, leaving little room for argument.

"Me too," announced Megan proudly.

Jack just sat there looking at his children. "You guys are great. I'm so proud of you," he said. "I've been trying to get through this mess by myself, and I haven't been a very good dad. It'll be a lot easier with your help."

"Will you go to church with us, Daddy?" asked Megan.

"We'll talk about that later," said Robby quickly, not wanting to lose the magic if the moment. "I have homework to do, and we have to clean up this kitchen."

The kids hadn't been in bed long when Jack heard the car in the driveway. "Why so early?" he asked, opening the door for Sally.

"Things were really slow, so they said if anyone wanted to leave early they could. I left before they could change their mind."

"Good for you. We have a lot to talk about," he said, starting to heat some water for the cup of tea he knew she wanted.

"Yes, we do. I want to hear all the details. Word for word."

He fixed her tea, took it in to her, and sat on the couch beside her. He told her the whole story, starting with his intention to sell his truck, to Don getting people to help get equipment over to Alice's house. Sally listened to Jack without interruption, sometimes amused, sometimes almost angry with him, sometimes almost brought to tears, hoping to remember all the many questions she wanted to ask.

"I can't begin to describe how I feel right now," she said when he was finished.

"Same here," said Jack.

"When are you going to figure out that Don is not your enemy?" asked Sally.

"I think I've got a handle on that," he said sheepishly.

"What if he would have walked away?" Jack just looked at her and said nothing.

Sally accepted that. "What do you think about what Pastor Scot said?"

"I don't know. I know I have a lot of things to be angry at my parents about, but it never occurred to me that I might be taking it out on the church. I really don't have time to deal with that right now," said Jack.

Or don't want to, thought Sally.

"Do you think you would ever sit down and talk to him about it?" Once again, Jack just sat there. "I'm asking you to please, seriously, give it some thought." *Time to move on,* thought Sally, after an uncomfortable silence.

"What did you think when Alice told you how much she would pay?"

"On the drive over to her house, I did the math. I thought if I could get around two thousand dollars, we could stall the bank off for maybe even a year. Then I thought I was being way too optimistic. When she said thirty-two fifty, I could barely speak. The weird thing is that she acted like she expected me to ask for more."

"What a feeling that must have been." Sally smiled. "I know how I felt when you told us. And then she has work for Robby."

"It was just one thing after another."

"Were you really going to let him go on the work mission?"

"Yes, as long as he did all the rest of the fundraisers. And I still expect him to do that."

"I'm sure he will without any argument," said Sally. "If you had trouble speaking when Alice told you the price, I'll bet you choked on that check she gave you."

"I'm just glad I didn't cry. I thought I was going to."

Sally snuggled against his chest. "We're going to make it, Jack."

"I think we will," he agreed, holding her close.

They sat there clinging to each other, thinking about the incredible events of the day. Soon Sally felt herself giving way to fatigue. "I'm falling asleep. Let's go to bed," she said.

"Not yet," said Jack. "I haven't told you the rest of the story."

"What?" she asked, sitting up.

He told her about his conversation with their kids after she left. She was crying by the time he finished. "You could have told me that first." She smiled through her tears. "Now I'll never get to sleep."

Robby was still struggling with his homework when he heard his mother come home. Unable to concentrate, he knew he was doing a poor job of it, but he had plugged away until all he had left was a chapter in his social studies book on reconstruction after the Civil War. He knew he would remember little of it the next day. He set his alarm and turned off the light, not expecting that he would go to sleep very soon.

He went back over everything that had happened at dinner, savoring it all. Their house was safe again; his dad had splurged on dinner, even bought ice cream. It was so good to see his mom happy; maybe soon she wouldn't have to work two jobs. And he was going on the work mission. He was sure now that his dad would have let him go anyway. That was the best part.

Then he thought about all the work they had to do. He knew his dad would want to work long hours to get Alice's house painted. When would he do all the stuff he already did, like shopping and fixing meals? He and Cassie would have to help. They could do the laundry and keep the house clean. He would talk to her about it tomorrow.

Then the all-too-familiar feeling of dread swept over him. He still had to own up to his parents about the quarters. The reason he took them in the first place wasn't a reason anymore. Things were going to be the way they were and everyone was going to be happy, but he was going to mess it up. He knew that Don would say nobody at the church would even know about their problems if Robby hadn't taken the quarters, and they would have found someone else to paint Alice's house. But his dad wouldn't accept that. He would be ashamed of him, and so would his mom. Mom might stop going to church, and his dad would never go. How could he go back there after everyone found out what he did? He had to tell them. Telling them couldn't be any worse than worrying about it all the time.

CHAPTER 15

Jack drove to the bank in a light mist, hoping it would be stopped by the time he was finished. The weather guessers had promised a dry day—partly sunny, partly cloudy with no chance of rain. *So much for dippler-doppler*, he thought sourly. When he came back out the mist had turned into a steady drizzle, doing nothing for his foul mood.

The teller at the counter couldn't figure out how to do the transaction, so he had to wait for the loan officer to get off the phone with a "client."

"All I want to do is make this month's payment plus all the penalties, and I'll deal with the other missed payments later in the month." Jack tried to be patient.

"You can't do it that way," the man said, offering no explanation.

"Why not?" *I should have just called Jeff and had him help me through this. Then I wouldn't have to be putting up with this jerk*, thought Jack.

"Because in order to catch up your account, you must pay in the same order in which you became delinquent." The man spoke in a patronizing tone.

Jack stared at him. "But then I'll have to pay a penalty for May."

The man shrugged. "That's the way it works."

So in the end, Jack was only able to make the February payment and four months of penalties, feeling very much put upon for having to pay a penalty for May. Plus, it was after nine thirty, and he didn't like making people wait who were going out of their way to help him.

The garage was around the back of the church behind the playground, just as Don had told him. The doors were up, and four men were inside having an animated conversation. To his relief, he saw that one of them was Don. He stopped the truck and got out to the sound of laughter. *Someone must have told a joke*, thought Jack.

Don walked toward the front of the garage to meet him. "Good morning, Jack. Everything go all right?"

"Not exactly," Jack answered, shaking Don's extended hand.

"Sorry to hear that," said Don, deciding not to ask any questions. "Let me introduce you to my friends Bob, Ed, and Mike. Guys, this is my friend Jack." *When did that happen?* thought Jack as he shook their hands.

"Sorry I'm so late," Jack apologized.

"We haven't been here that long," said Ed.

"Looks like you won't be doing any painting today anyway," said Bob.

"We can always count on those weather guys to keep us safe," cracked Mike.

"This rain doesn't look like it's going away, so we'll come back tomorrow and get this stuff over to Alice's," said Don.

"On Saturday?" Jack asked.

They all looked at each other. "Saturday is just another day to us old guys," said Ed, getting nods of agreement all around.

"Nine o'clock again?" asked Mike.

Everybody agreed. "Will you bring Robby?" Don asked.

"If I can get him up. Saturday is not just another day to him," Jack answered to a chorus of chuckles.

"Robby's a good kid," said Mike.

"Mike's going on the work mission," Don said to Jack. "I told him if he wanted good help to get Robby on his crew."

"I've already submitted my list to Jay," said Mike.

"Good luck with that," said Bob.

They all hurried out in the rain to their cars. Don hung back with Jack. "Mike is the perfect guy for Robby to work with on his first work mission," he said.

"Thanks. I assume you made that happen."

"Maybe," said Don. "I assume you had problems at the bank."

Jack told him the story. "If I ever get the chance, I'm going to refinance with another bank," said Jack.

"Don't blame you. But you're still better off than you were yesterday."

"I know that," said Jack.

Robby went straight home from school, did all of his homework, and then started making a list of all the things he and his sisters could do around the house so their dad could get his job done faster. He was still working on it when Cassie came home. He explained his idea to her and showed her what he had thought of so far.

"I think painting that house is going to take a long time," he told her. "If we can help Dad get done quicker, maybe he can get done in time to catch up on the payments before we have to pay another penalty."

"What about helping with the painting? Wouldn't that make it go faster?"

"You know Dad. He'll work till dark and then come home and try to do everything else. That's okay for those little one day jobs he does, but this is going to be every day for a while, and it just won't work."

Cassie remembered a few nights when they didn't eat until eight o'clock and their mom had to come home to an unhappy family. "Okay, but what about your job for Alice?"

"I don't know how much there is to it, but I hope I can get it done tomorrow."

"We."

"Right, we."

Just then Jack pushed through the door with his arms full of groceries. "There're more in the truck if you guys—" Robby and Cassie were out of the door before he could finish. *Whose kids are those?* he thought to himself.

They filed back in with Megan trudging behind them, already loaded down with her backpack. "I got the last one," she proclaimed proudly, holding up a bag with one item in it.

They started to help Jack put the groceries away. "Are you guys all right?" he asked.

"Yeah. We need to talk," said Robby.

"Sounds ominous."

"It's not," said Cassie, giving him a twelve-year-old attitude look.

They told him their ideas and then waited anxiously while he digested it all. "First, I want you to know how proud I am of you for the way have been understanding about our family's problems. The thing I want to avoid right now is putting any more burden on your mother. She's been carrying a big load for over a year now, and she'll try to take on even more if we don't stop her. I have three weeks to catch up the loan without paying another penalty. If you guys could help on Saturdays and do the things that need to be done at home during the week, I think I can make it."

"Do you have to work long hours?" asked Cassie.

"I won't at first, but if it looks like I'm running out of time, I will. The rain today didn't help matters any."

"What about tomorrow?" asked Robby.

"Tomorrow you and I are meeting those guys at the church and taking the ladders and scaffold over to Alice's."

"What about us?" said Cassie, looking at Megan.

"Well, I thought you could do some chores, spend time with your mother, and then have her bring you to Alice's after lunch on her way to work. By then we should have the equipment over there and set up ready to work. And Robby will probably know what all he has to do as well."

That seemed to satisfy Cassie. "Okay," she said.

CHAPTER 16

Jack and Robby woke up the next day to more overcast skies, but it didn't look like it would rain. They packed their lunches then loaded what painting and yard tools they thought they would need in the truck and headed for the church. As they drove into the parking lot, Robby noticed that the sky had actually brightened a little bit. *All we need is more rain-outs*, he thought. They saw only two other cars there, Bob and Mike standing beside them talking.

"Good morning, Jack," they said, shaking hands.

"What's that following you?" asked Bob as Robby came around the back of the truck. Robby just grinned. Bob gave him a one-armed hug. Bob was one of the first persons who took an interest in him when he started coming to church. Don had told Robby that it was Bob who had found the quarter tube where Robby had hidden it. *Just one more person who will be disappointed in me*, he thought.

Just then Ed drove in, and before he could get parked so did Don. They put the scaffolding on Bob's truck and the ladders on Mike's. By ten o'clock they had everything loaded and tied down. The sky had turned noticeably darker again, and Jack was watching it anxiously.

"Don't worry about it," said Mike. "Bluster Bill said no chance of rain today."

"That's what Raingage Robert said yesterday, and look what happened," Bob chimed in.

"Stormcheck Stan said it could perhaps maybe possibly or not; we would just have to wait and see, and he would tell us what it did tomorrow," Ed finished it off.

Unable to think of anything clever to add, Don said, "Let's go before it does—if it's going to."

They unloaded the trucks and started to assemble the scaffold next to one of the dormers on the side of the house. After a while Alice came out to watch. They all greeted her, and she smiled and waved to them. Bob went over to talk to her.

"Is that the boy?" she asked, referring to Robby, who was holding up a piece of scaffold while Ed and Mike pinned the cross-bracing to it.

"Yep, that's him," Bob answered.

"Kind of scrawny, isn't he? Don't they feed him?"

Bob laughed. "That's all he does is eat," said Bob, waving Robby over.

Robby waited until the scaffold was secure and then walked over to Alice and Bob. "Alice, this is your new landscaper, Robby. Robby, this is … what should he call you?" asked Bob.

She gave Bob a condescending look. "Well, my name is Alice."

"Hi … Alice," said Robby tentatively, not sure how to take her. Bob just grinned and walked away shaking his head.

"Hello, Robby. Are you ready to go to work?" she asked, watching Bob go with just a hint of a smile.

"Yes," he answered.

"Have you ever done this before?" she asked as they walked over to the side of the garage.

Robby looked at the tangled snarl of bushes and vines that had grown about eight feet tall. "No, but I've watched my dad do it at our house," he said. "But he never let it get this bad," he added, regretting his words before they were out of his mouth.

After an uncomfortable pause, Alice said, "Well, I hope you watched closely because I want it done right." Her face showed no sign that she was offended by his remark.

"It will be. If I'm not sure about something, I'll ask my dad."

"Well, get started."

"Okay, I'll get the tools out of my dad's truck. How low do you want them cut?"

"Cut those bushes down to about four feet and clean out all of the dead stuff. And pull out all those wild morning glories, roots and all," she told him.

"Where do I put the brush?" he asked as she walked away.

"Just out in front of the garage for now," she answered without turning around. "But don't block the door."

Robby headed over to his dad's truck and started unloading the tools, trying to figure out if Alice was unhappy with him or not. "How did that go?" Don startled him.

Robby slumped his shoulders. "I'm not sure," he exhaled.

"Alice is a nice woman, Robby. It might seem like she's mad about something, but she isn't. Maybe a little sour, but not mad. She speaks her mind and doesn't apologize for it. Part of the way she is, is because she's lonely. But you will end up liking her."

"I hope so." He sighed.

The scaffold was erected by eleven o'clock, and Jack was ready to actually start working on the house. The sun had been popping its face through the clouds occasionally, and all worry of rain was gone. Bob, Mike, and Dan all took shots at the weather guessers as they left. Don stopped in to say something to Alice before going. Jack thanked them all profusely, genuinely grateful for all their help. They insisted that he let them know when he needed to move the scaffold and they would help him.

Just before noon, Jack climbed down from the scaffold and walked back to check on Robby's progress. He could see the side of the garage from the scaffold, so he had been keeping an eye on him anyway. Jack was pleased to see that Robby was working steadily and making some progress.

"Looking good," said Jack, inspecting his son's work approvingly.

"Thanks." Robby grinned. "How's that going?" he asked, nodding toward the house.

"More scraping than I expected, and there are some places where I'm going to have to caulk. How about some lunch?"

"I'm starved."

"Imagine that," said Jack, going to the truck to get the cooler. Robby added an armload of brush to the top of his pile.

There was a small, weather-beaten picnic table near the back of the house that looked as though it hadn't been used for a long time. "What do you think of Alice?" Jack asked.

"Not sure," answered Robby through a mouthful of sandwich. "Don said we'll get used to her and we'll like her. What did you think of those guys?"

Jack wasn't sure how to say it. "Listening to them jab at each other all the time made me dizzy. But they're friends; they like each other. I can't imagine my dad fitting in with those guys. And they got all that work done."

Robby grinned. "So you liked them."

"Yes, I did," said Jack honestly.

Alice appeared at the back door. "You're welcome to come inside; you don't have to eat at that dirty old table."

"No, thanks," said Jack. "It's a nice day to eat outside."

"Suit yourselves." And she was gone.

Jack looked at Robby. "Don said that she's lonely," said Robby. "Maybe we should have gone in."

They heard voices and looked up to see Sally, Cassie, and Megan come around the corner of the house. "You guys still eating?" asked Cassie, helping herself to some potato chips.

"We're just finishing up. You guys are early," said Jack, getting up and giving his wife a kiss.

"I wanted have time to look at what you were doing," said Sally.

Jack started packing the cooler back up. Robby stuck a banana in his pocket and grabbed one last handful of chips before his father could get to them. Jack took them on a tour around the house. They were headed back to Robby's project when Alice came out the back door.

"Alice, come and meet the rest of my family," said Jack. "This is my wife, Sally, and my daughters, Cassie and Megan."

"I'm happy to meet you, Alice," said Sally, shaking her hand.

"Hi," said Cassie.

"Hello, Miss Alice," said Megan in her most grown-up voice and reached out her hand.

Alice shook her hand and said, "Well, hello to you, Miss Megan. It's nice to meet you all. I'm keeping your menfolks busy."

"And us too," said Megan.

"And how is that?" Alice was puzzled.

"We're going to help Robby so he can get done quicker and help our dad," said Cassie. Megan nodded in agreement.

Alice turned to Sally. "And what are you going to do?"

"I'm going to work."

Alice turned back to the girls. "Your brother needs to earn his money for that mission trip by himself. He's doing just fine, and there's no hurry in getting the house painted. You want to do something, I need help in the house," she said, starting toward the house. "Come along."

Sally gave Jack a "What is going on?" look. Jack shrugged and motioned with his hand for them to follow her. "Let's you and me get back to work," he said to Robby. Robby watched with amusement as his confused mother and sisters went into the house with Alice.

Alice trundled on through her kitchen. "Sit there at the table." She motioned without turning around. They sat down and could hear her rummaging around in the dining room. She came back carrying an old wooden box that looked like a large jewelry box. She placed it in the table, sat down, raised the lid, and carefully folded it back on the table so the loose hinges wouldn't pull out.

"I can't do this anymore because of the arthritis in my hands," she said, holding up two blackened spoons. "This is my mother's silverware. It's almost one hundred years old."

Sally took the spoons from her and looked at the finely crafted flowers and leaves embossed on the handles. *Beautiful*, she thought. It was something she had always wanted. "I think you guys get to clean these," Sally said to her girls.

"I forgot the polish," Alice grumbled to herself. She started to push herself up out of her chair and then thought better of it. "Megan, there's a jar of silver polish in there on my hutch. Will you get it for me please?"

"Sure," said Megan and was there and back before Alice could have gotten out of her chair.

She showed them how to dab the polish on the rag and gently massage it onto the spoon, revealing the beauty of the silver.

"Wow," said Megan.

"Awesome," said Cassie.

"I did that in the easy spoon part; the rest of it doesn't go that fast," she told them. "When you finish that spoon, you'll be able to see your reflection in it."

She gave them both small, soft rags, and they each eagerly attacked a spoon. It became obvious to Sally that she had become a fifth wheel. She really wanted to stay and watch her children interact with this unusual woman, but she had to go to work. "I'd better go," she announced.

"See ya, Mom," they chorused, barely looking up from what they were doing.

"Come back again," said Alice, "when you don't have to run off so soon."

"I'll do that." Sally smiled, meaning it. She went outside, waved good-bye to Robby, blew Jack a kiss, and headed for work. *I like her*, she thought. *She could be the grandmother my kids never had.*

After a couple of hours of asking question about each other Alice said, "We should take a break. And so should your dad and brother. Are you thirsty?"

They both nodded. "Megan, you go fetch those men, and Cassie and I will start making lemonade."

Megan walked back to where Robby was working. "I'm fetching you." She grinned.

"What?"

"Alice told me to go fetch the men. We're having lemonade." Megan laughed. "She says some funny things."

They called for their dad to come down, and they all went in to have lemonade. The girls showed Jack and Robby what they were doing and made them look at their reflections in the shiny spoons. Robby drained his second glass of lemonade, and Alice pushed the pitcher over his way, indicating that he was welcome to have more, which he did.

"They say you don't go to church with them," Alice said to Jack. Robby and Cassie exchanged nervous glances.

Jack pursed his lips. "No, I don't," he said quietly, knowing that wouldn't be the end of it.

"Seems like it wouldn't hurt you to go with them, at least once in a while."

Jack wasn't going to respond to that. He was going to get up and go back to work before he said the wrong thing. "You might want to be careful if you do, though." They all wanted to ask why. They waited for her to tell them. "It might just sneak up on you."

Robby was just taking a big gulp of lemonade and had to choke half of it back into his glass, making a mess all over the table. Cassie and Megan were convulsed in laughter. Jack just sat there with his eyes closed, wishing he were somewhere else.

"There's a dishrag in the sink. I'm not cleaning up your mess," Alice said pleasantly.

"And then we're going back to work," said Jack, ending the conversation. He put his empty glass on the counter, thanked Alice for the lemonade, and went out the door.

No one said anything while Robby cleaned up the table. He was almost out the door when he turned back and said to Alice, "Thanks for saying that." Alice gave him an understanding smile.

Just before five, Alice and the girls came outside. Robby and Jack were starting to put away their tools. Alice walked around, inspecting their work. "Can I get you to cut about another foot off those bushes?" she said to Robby. "I thought that was where I wanted them, but they don't look right."

"Sure," said Robby, relieved to know that she didn't think he had cut them to the wrong height. "Is it okay if I leave my tools in the garage?"

"If there's room." She made a wry face. "It's unlocked."

Robby raised the door and stared at a mountain of boxes, bags, furniture, and other stuff he couldn't identify. It was stacked to within inches of the door.

Alice looked at Robby. "That's our next project," she said. "All trash is in two weeks, and I want to get rid of most of that stuff."

"What's all trash?" asked Cassie.

"All trash is when you put all the trash you have at the curb and the city picks it up."

"Unlimited pick up," Jack explained.

"Ooh," said Cassie and Robby.

Alice shook her head and ambled off toward the scaffold. Robby found a spot to put his tools and carefully lowered the garage door.

"You got some paint on," she said to Jack, looking up at the dormer. "Do you like the color?"

"Doesn't matter. It's your house."

She looked at him with a slight frown. "It would be nice to know if other people thought your house looked nice."

"Well, I like it," announced Megan in her most important voice, striking a pose and folding her arms across her chest.

"I like the gray much better than that old brown," said Cassie.

"Even if I didn't like it, I wouldn't say so," said Robby, getting a slap on the arm from Cassie.

"You're smarter than you look," said Alice, causing loud giggles from Megan and Cassie.

"I want to get the trim on the dormer before I move the scaffold, so you'll get to see what that looks like tomorrow," said Jack.

"Monday," said Alice.

Jack's face fell. "I can't work on Sunday?"

"Not here." Her jaw was set.

Letting out a big sigh, Jack said, "Monday it is, then. Does it matter how early?"

"Not to me."

"You didn't tell us if you like the color." Jack smiled, opening the door to his truck.

"I think I do." She smiled back.

The kids said good-bye, thanked Alice for everything, and piled into the truck. She waved to them as they drove away. *Nice kids*, she said to herself. *He's not as tough as he thinks he is.*

CHAPTER 17

On Wednesday, Robby had so much to tell Don he hardly had time to eat. He had started talking while he was getting in the van and had only stopped a few times since. Now he was finishing a cold taco, only his second. Way below his average.

"But the bad part is that it rained again, and my dad is worried about getting done in time to catch up the mortgage without another penalty. He barely worked half the morning on Monday and not at all on Tuesday. He hopes he can completely finish the dormer today."

"If he does, he'll need to move the scaffold. You tell him we'll come over in the morning and help him do that. We're all meeting at the church tomorrow anyway," said Don. "And I think Alice will make sure he has enough money to fix your mortgage even if he's not quite finished."

"I hope so. I'm really starting to like her. My sisters think she's awesome. She told them stories about when she was little, and she uses a lot of old fashioned words that they think are funny. And she gave them each ten dollars for sitting there rubbing a rag on spoons and forks."

Don listened to the continuous narrative with great amusement. The whole family had obviously greatly enjoyed the day, even Jack, in spite of himself. "Sounds like a great day," said Don, "but I'll bet it was the greatest for Alice."

"Doesn't she have any family?"

"No, she took care of sick parents for many, many years in that very house and never was married. She can't drive anymore and has to depend on people from church to take her to the store or the doctor or wherever."

"I'll bet my mom would take her to the store," said Robby. "If she ever had the time," he added glumly.

"When are you going back?"

"Not till Saturday. My dad offered to get me from school, but he'd have to put all his stuff away and then get it out again. It just didn't seem like it was worth it. Didn't matter anyway so far. So I just go home and help around the house and work on supper."

"Not much time for Robby."

"I go on Sunday nights." Robby shrugged. "And I help Jay do stuff for the fundraisers, but no." Then he grinned. "Except for Wednesdays."

"It's been fun, hasn't it?

"Yeah. Only two more weeks of school." Robby seemed sad.

"And barely two weeks after that the work mission." Robby didn't say anything. "You've got to tell them."

"I know." He sighed. "Jay said I should tell them before the work mission."

"I agree," said Don, "but I think you can wait until school is out."

"Sometimes I get the urge to just blurt it out and get it over with."

"No harm in that. When the time comes, God will put the right words in your mouth."

"Like he did when I told Alice how much of a mess her bushes were in?"

Don laughed. "No, you get all the credit for that."

They picked up Cassie, and Don got to hear the Alice stories all over again. And it all came out faster than when Robby told it. "And she doesn't get mad when we laugh at the funny things she says. I think she does some of it on purpose."

"That could be entirely possible," Don agreed. "I'm sure she is enjoying your company very much."

Don dropped them off in their driveway. Not seeing Jack's truck, he reminded Robby to tell his dad that they would help him with the scaffold in the morning.

Jack was scraping the house on the extension ladder when his help arrived. Don, Bob, and Mike got out of Don's van, along with someone Jack didn't know.

"You do nice work," said Bob, inspecting the dormer.

"Do you like the color?" asked Alice, sticking her nose out the door.

"It's okay," said Bob.

"It's your house, Alice. You can paint it any color you want," said the man Jack didn't know. Jack laughed harder than he had in a long time.

"I give up," snorted Alice and shut the door.

"I got in trouble for saying that," he said, still chuckling on his way down the ladder.

Jack shook hands all around. "I'm Joe," said the new man.

"Thanks for backing me up," said Jack.

"If we didn't give her a hard time, Alice would think we didn't like her," said Don. "Before we leave, we will all compliment her on her color selection."

"Where are you going next with the scaffold?" asked Bob.

"I think I'll do the dormer on the driveway side," said Jack.

Jack lowered the scaffold down to them piece by piece, listening to the same friendly banter between them he had enjoyed on Saturday. They left the bottom section intact and collectively carried it around to the other side of the house. They were just sitting it in place when Alice came out to see what was going on.

"I wouldn't have thought you guys could agree on anything long enough to move that thing in the same direction at once," said Jack.

"Oh, listen to the new guy," said Mike. "Thinks he's funny." Jack got the reaction he was hoping for.

"I've got good role models," he deadpanned.

"No argument there." Alice couldn't stay out of it. "I think you're going to be all right," she said to Jack, who was enjoying being part of the fun.

After they reassembled the scaffold to its full height, Mike said to Jack, "We're going back to the church for coffee. Why don't you join us?"

"Thanks, but I'd better stick with it," said Jack, really wishing he could go.

"You have to take a break sometime," said Joe.

"I know, but you guys have already slowed me down enough for one day."

"See if we ever help him again," said Bob.

"If you boys could ever stop your bickering, I've already made coffee and I've got cookies, so you don't have to go anywhere," said Alice.

"Are the cookies homemade?" asked Don.

Alice stuck her nose in the air and started for the house. "See for yourself," she sniffed.

They all piled into her kitchen and made room around the table. Alice passed out cups and handed them the coffee pot to pass around. Then she put out a big plate of cookies—homemade chocolate chip cookies with nuts.

Jack's urgent need to keep working faded away as he felt himself being absorbed into the camaraderie of the group. He thought about what was happening. He thought back to how it was when he was forced to go to church. He could remember mean faces snarling at him, but he didn't see any of those faces around the table with him. *Why am I hanging out with people I've spent most of my life trying to avoid?*

"We better get going," he heard someone say, bringing him back into focus. They all thanked Alice for the coffee and cookies and complimented her on her choice of paint.

"I had to bribe you to get you to say it," she chided them.

That night Robby waited until Sally had finished her dinner and had a chance to relax. She had worked until seven, and he knew she would be tired, but he wanted to talk to her. She was sitting on the couch reading a book, drinking a cup of tea. Jack was still doing something in the kitchen.

"Hi, Robby." Sally smiled, looking up from her book.

"Can I talk to you about something?"

"Of course; is something wrong?" She laid her book on the end table.

"No, it's about Alice." Jack came in the room and sat beside his wife. "Don told me that she doesn't have any family and the only way she gets to the store or anywhere is if someone from church takes her. She never asks anyone; she just waits for someone to call to see if she needs anything."

"I wondered about that," said Jack.

"I know how much you work and how busy you are, but—"

"I'd love to, Robby. I like Alice. It would be fun to take her shopping."

"I didn't think it would be that easy," said Robby.

"I didn't mean to disappoint you." Sally laughed. "I have been thinking about just going to visit her, but your idea is better."

The next day was a rare day off for Sally and she had planned to do some shopping anyway. So they talked it over and came up with a plan. Sally would spend the first part of the day relaxing and doing little things she hadn't had time for. Then she would pick Robby, Cassie, and Megan up from school and go over to Alice's. Robby could work on the bushes and come home with his dad, and all the women would go shopping.

"I'll call Alice in the morning and make sure she wants to go," said Sally.

Robby listened to his sisters jabber about how much fun it was going to be taking Alice shopping. *I'd rather clean my room four times than do that*, he thought. They pulled into the driveway, and there was Alice, sitting in a lawn chair, all dressed up with her purse in her lap, watching Jack paint. Robby got out and held the door while Alice got in. They all hollered something to Jack, who was up on a ladder, and then off they went.

"You sure you didn't want to go with them?" Jack asked, trying to sound serious.

Robby spied a glove on the ground and threw it at his father, missing badly. "You're making good progress," he said.

"Don't jinx me; I haven't had one problem all day. Did they say when they would be back?"

"Mom said she fixed supper in the crock pot, and we could eat whenever we wanted and don't worry about them," said Robby, opening his dad's cooler to see if there was anything left over from lunch.

"I'd like to work a little later, then, if you don't mind," said Jack, continuing to paint, his back to Robby.

"I don't mind," said Robby as he bit into half of a sandwich and stuffed an apple in his pocket.

"There's stuff left from lunch in the cooler if you get hungry."

"Too late." Robby laughed.

Jack turned around and saw Robby holding up what was left of the sandwich. "I should have known to pack two lunches." He shook his head and went back to his painting.

Robby polished off the sandwich and opened the garage door to get his tools, savoring the good feeling of horseplay with his dad. Right on the heels of that, his all-too-frequent companion crept into his consciousness. Would there be more moments like that after he made his confession? He tried to put it back out of his mind. The good feeling was gone.

Cassie and Megan were having more fun watching Alice poke around in stores she'd never been in than they were shopping for themselves. Sally had driven to the new mall south of town at the request of her daughters. After about an hour, Sally noticed that Alice was getting tired.

"Maybe we should stop and rest a while," said Sally.

"We could sit on those benches over there by the fountain," suggested Megan. "And Cassie and I could go over there," she said, pointing beyond the fountain, with an impish grin on her face, "and get smoothies for all of us."

Sally knew she was trapped. "What's a smoothie?" asked Alice.

"Oh, they're sooo good," said Cassie. "They have a million flavors."

"Like what?"

Cassie and Megan took turns reciting them.

"Mango Magic."

"Blimey Limey."

"Rockin' Raspberry—really good."

"Sunny Day."

"Okay, we get the picture," Sally interrupted, digging in her purse for money.

"Nonsense," said Alice, "it will be my treat." Sally started to protest, but the set of Alice's jaw changed her mind.

"Would you mind stopping at a grocery on the way home so I could get a few things?" Alice asked Sally while the girls were off getting their drinks.

"Of course not; I have to pick up a few things as well," Sally answered. "Do you have a regular day when you go shopping?"

"No, I just go whenever someone offers to take me."

"We should set up a time to go every week."

"With your work schedule?" Alice looked at her over the top of her glasses.

"Alice, shopping is therapy for me, and I would love to have your company."

Alice looked away and put her hand over her mouth to stop her chin from trembling. Sally was relieved to see the girls walking up with the drinks.

"There was no line," said Megan, "so we didn't have to wait. We got you Rockin' Raspberry—raspberries, strawberries, and bananas." She handed a drink to Alice.

"I can't drink all that," said Alice, regaining her composure. "Why didn't you get me a small?"

"They don't have smalls." Cassie shrugged. "They only have regular and large."

"We won't finish ours either," explained Megan. "We put them in the freezer and have them the next day."

"Or maybe tonight." Cassie giggled, giving her mother a side-long look.

While they were waiting in the checkout line at the grocery, Alice suddenly announced, "You better start thinking about a place to eat." They all looked at her. "You don't think I'm going to go home and eat by myself, do you?" Cassie and Megan picked Panera Bread.

During the meal, Alice entertained them with stories of when she was young. Out of the blue, Megan looked at her and asked, "How old are you?"

Sally held her breath. "It's not polite to ask someone their age," said Alice.

"You asked us how old we are."

"I did, but that's different."

"Why?" Megan furrowed her brow.

Unable to think of a reason that would make sense to an eight-year-old, Alice said, "Eighty- three."

Megan's eyes got big, and she looked at Sally. "Is that really old?"

Alice couldn't stop herself from laughing. "Yes, Megan, that's really old."

Sally realized she was still holding her breath. She couldn't decide who was having more fun, her girls or Alice. Or herself. "We should get home; I've hardly seen your dad for two days."

"Thank you all for putting up with me for so long," said Alice on the drive to her house.

"We didn't put up with you." Megan was indignant.

"I had fun," said Cassie.

"So did I," said Alice. "I can't remember when I've had such good company."

Later that evening Jack and Sally sat at the kitchen table telling each other about their day. Robby was playing games on the computer, and the girls were watching television.

They had argued briefly about bedtime because the next day was Saturday, until Jack reminded them they still had to get up early if they wanted to go with him to Alice's.

"I think the girls have made a real connection with Alice," said Sally. "She's not as stuffy as she'd like you to think. Megan really loosened her up."

"What about Sally?"

"What do you mean?"

"Have you made a connection with Alice? How old would your mother be?" asked Jack.

"I've thought about that. Mom would have been eighty-two in August." Sally looked sad.

"Go for it. I'm sure she'd like the attention."

"How are you getting along with her?"

Jack wrinkled his nose. "Okay. She seems satisfied with my work, but she's not very long on compliments. And she hasn't said any more about me going to church."

"I'll remind her," teased Sally.

"Not funny."

"But the subject doesn't upset you anymore."

"I am kind of wondering about Robby, though." Jack changed the subject.

Sally was caught off guard. "What about Robby?"

"I'm not sure, but I just sense that something's bothering him."

"Like what?"

"I don't know." Jack frowned. "It seems like he's just ready to tell me something and then doesn't. And sometimes he suddenly gets a sad, melancholy look. Right after you left this afternoon, we were laughing and goofing around with each other. A short time later I noticed him leaning on the rake just staring into space. Then he shook his head and went back to work."

"Why haven't I noticed any of that?" Sally wondered.

Jack shrugged. "I've been around him more that usual because of this job. I actually started noticing it right at the time we got the foreclosure notice. It's sudden and for short periods of time. Otherwise he seems fine."

"Why don't you just ask him if something is bothering him?" Sally suggested.

"I've been planning to, but I wanted to see what you thought first."

Sally reached for his hand across the table. "Now you've got me worried. Talk to him the next time it happens."

"I will," he promised.

CHAPTER 18

Robby had just finished raking up the last of the brush in the far corner of Alice's yard when he saw a brown pickup back up the driveway and stop at his brush pile. He picked up an armload from the ground, walked across the yard, and threw it on top of the pile.

Mike and another man got out and looked hard at the brush pile. "Looks like you've been busy," said Mike.

"Yeah," said Robby, raking some stray branches onto the pile.

"Robby, this is Butch. We're going to get this brush out of your way." Butch and Robby shook hands. "We'll never get it all in one load, though."

Fifteen minutes later they had the truck packed full, and Butch started lashing the load down with bungee cords and ropes. "Will you need help unloading it?" asked Alice, who had just returned from inspecting Robby's work along the back fence.

"No," said Mike, "the guys from the city unload it right into the chipper. We just sit and watch them."

"This boy cut out places I didn't even know needed it. Looks good, doesn't it?" said Alice, patting Robby on the shoulder.

"Yes, it does." said Butch. "From the looks of this pile, I can't believe he's been doing much standing around." The compliments made Robby uncomfortable. He didn't think he'd worked that hard.

"He's just getting in shape for the work mission," said Mike, grinning at Robby. "He knows I'm going to ride him hard." Robby grinned back, wondering how serious he was.

"Can you get the rest of it in one more load?" asked Alice.

Mike looked at what was left of the pile and then back at what Robby still had to bring over. "What do you think?" he asked Robby.

"I think we can get it all in if Alice doesn't want me to cut anything more down."

"I was hoping to get you to trim that maple tree up some, but I don't want to make you take a third load," said Alice.

"What if we load the rest of the brush and if we have any room left, Robby can trim branches until the truck is full," offered Butch.

"Fair enough," agreed Alice. Butch and Mike climbed back into the truck.

Alice patted Butch on the arm. "Thank you both for doing this."

Butch drove off, and Robby started to the back of the yard. "Do you want to start on that garage today?" Alice asked him.

Robby looked perplexed. "We don't have to, but I have to get it done by next week," said Alice.

"I had another idea." Robby grimaced.

Alice waited. "I think it's a pretty big job," he started. "I talked to Jay about it, and he wondered if we could make it a group project."

"What kind of group?"

"Well, there are some other kids who still want to earn more money for the trip, and I thought maybe they could help."

Alice thought it over. "I'll take two more," she said finally. "But that's all. I need time to look at everything to decide what to do with it, so only two more."

"Thanks." A relieved Robby grinned. "I'll tell Jay. Can we do it next Saturday?"

"As long as we get it all done. The following Tuesday is when they pick it all up," she said and went back into the house.

Robby finished cleaning up the brush and then helped his dad with the scraping while he waited for Butch and Mike to come back. He told Jack about the deal he had just made with Alice.

"I'd like to be done by then," said Jack.

"Do you think you can?" It didn't look like it to Robby.

"If it doesn't rain and no other jobs pop up, I think I have a chance. I'd like to get paid and get the loan straightened out."

Butch and Mike soon returned, and there was enough room on the truck to get the branches Alice wanted trimmed in the load. Just as they were ready to leave, Jack came down from the ladder. Mike introduced him to Butch.

"Do you guys ever do anything for yourselves?" Jack asked them.

"You sound like our wives." Butch laughed, as he got in the truck.

"Are you going to need to move that scaffold again?" asked Mike.

"No, I think I can get the rest off of the ladders. It sure made that part easier, though," Jack answered.

"We'll come over Thursday and get it out of your way," said Mike, joining Butch in the truck.

"If someone just helps me tear it down, I can get it back to the church."

"We'll talk about it Thursday." And they drove away.

Jack watched them go, not moving or saying anything. Finally he slapped his scraper against his leg and tossed it over by the ladder. "Let's eat," he said and went to the hose to wash his hands.

Robby got the cooler from the truck, trying to figure out his dad's mood. After Robby washed his hands, they went to the back door, and Jack knocked lightly. "It's open," a voice called from somewhere inside.

"We didn't want to just barge in on you, Alice," said Jack. He had been having lunch with her, and she had told him he didn't have to knock.

"What did you think you'd catch me doing?" Alice frowned.

"I don't know," said Jack, "sneaking a sip of the cooking wine, maybe."

She scowled at him and started getting her lunch together. "Did those fellows get all the brush on that last load?" she asked with her head stuck in the refrigerator.

"Yeah," said Robby "and we got that tree trimmed like you wanted it too."

"Good." She came out of the refrigerator smiling. "One more thing I've been intending to get done. Maybe I should hire you."

Robby just looked at her.

"The boy that cuts my grass is graduating from high school and has a full-time job for the summer. He's quitting in two weeks. You interested?"

"Yeah," said Robby. "Sure I am."

"He's always kept it cut the way I want it, but I can never get him to do anything else I need done. Like trim that tree. Or keep those bushes cut down."

"I'll do anything you want." Robby shrugged.

"It takes about an hour and fifteen minutes to mow and trim, and I pay him fifteen dollars. That all right with you?"

Robby looked at Jack and got no help whatsoever. *He's going to make me decide this myself.* "That's fine," he said.

"Any extra jobs I have we'll argue about the pay."

"I'm sure you'll be fair, Alice," Jack spoke up. *I guess that means he thinks the fifteen dollars is fair,* thought Robby.

"I've got a mower somewhere in the garage that I think still works. You're welcome to it. I'll furnish the gas."

"When you guys empty the garage next week, I'll check it out," said Jack. "I'll take it home and change the oil and put a new spark plug in it."

They heard a clatter of voices coming around the back of the house. "Knock, knock," said Cassie, walking through the door, followed by Megan and Sally.

"Come in, come in," said Alice, happy to see them.

"We came to help," announced Megan.

"Oh, I'll have to think of something for you to do," said Alice. She hadn't been expecting them.

"We came to help Dad and Robby," said Cassie. Cassie was worried about Jack getting paid in time to get the mortgage caught up and had insisted that Sally bring them over to help. Jack had tried to reassure her several times that he would get done in time to stop the foreclosure, but she would not be mollified.

"I'd rather help Alice," said Megan.

"If Alice needs help with something, maybe you could get that done first," said Sally.

Cassie's eyes pleaded with her mother. "But what if we don't get done—"

"Cassie," Jack interrupted gently, "I've got it all worked out, and there is no need to worry."

"What if you don't get done? Is there a hurry? Are you going somewhere?" asked Alice, clearly puzzled and concerned for Cassie.

Jack sighed and slumped his shoulders. "Our house is under foreclosure, and Cassie is afraid it we'll lose it before we can catch up on the payments. But it won't happen that fast."

"You need money to keep your house from being foreclosed, and you didn't tell me?" Alice was rapidly moving from puzzled and concerned to angry.

"You already paid me money in advance, and I'm not finished," Jack protested.

"I could pay you for what you have done. Probably should have anyway. How much do you need?" Alice had a twinge of remorse for not offering to pay him as he finished the work.

"Almost all of it. If you don't catch up all the way, they won't stop the process. Which is why I didn't ask for money along the way."

"But, Dad—" Robby blurted out and then stopped himself. Alice looked from Robby to Jack.

"Go on, Robby," said Jack. "But what?" The tone of Jack's voice told Robby it was all right to say what was on his mind.

"What about the penalties?"

"You're right; there will be more penalties if we go past the grace period."

"When is that?" asked Alice.

"Unfortunately, it's Monday," said Jack.

"I want to make sure I understand this," said Alice. "If you bring the loan up-to-date on Monday, they have to drop all foreclosure action, and you will avoid more penalties. And that will amount to most of what I owe you."

"That's correct."

Alice thought for a while. "You find out exactly how much it will take, and I'll give you a check Monday morning. Then I'll pay you the rest of it when you're completely finished. And you, young lady"—she looked sternly at Cassie—"you stop worrying. Your father is not going to let the bank take your house. You're too young and too pretty to have a worried look on your face."

She turned back to Jack. "I don't want to see you with a paintbrush in your hand on Monday until everything is settled with the bank." Alice had taken over.

Jack's mind was in conflict. Part of him wanted to tell her to stay out of it, and part of him wanted to just accept the offer and not rock the boat, but most of him wanted to thank this quirky old woman for caring so much for his family, which she obviously did. And she had become important to them too.

Sally, who had been listening nervously to all of this, let out a long sigh. "I have to go to work, Jack." He looked at her questioningly. "I want to know what you're going to do before I go."

Jack phrased his answer carefully. "I want to know what you want to do, so *we* can decide what to do."

Trying to keep the quiver out of her voice, Sally said, "I want you to take Monday morning off." Jack saw vigorous nods of agreement from his children.

Megan broke the tension. "Does that mean I get to help Alice this afternoon?"

Sally picked up her purse and gave Alice a look of gratitude. "I'll call you about shopping," she said.

"Please do."

Robby, Cassie, and Megan sat down at the old picnic table while Jack walked Sally to the car. Sally took Jack's hand and continued to hold it as they faced each other at the car.

"Did you almost get mad in there?"

"Almost. But it's hard to be angry at someone who has adopted your family," Jack answered.

"I don't want to upset you," said Sally carefully, "but I want you to think about something. You don't have to agree with me, but I want you to think about it. All of these things that are happening to us in the past few weeks are happening because our kids became connected with the church. I have to go." She gave him a quick kiss and got into the car. "I love you," she threw out the window as she drove away.

"I love you too," Jack said to the disappearing car and then trudged back to his waiting children.

Before Jack could say anything, Cassie spoke up. "Dad, I'm sorry, I didn't mean to cause trouble."

Jack gave her a hug and kissed her on the forehead. "It turns out, Cassie, that you fixed a problem."

"Did Mom tell you to say that?"

"No." Jack chuckled. "We didn't even discuss it."

"What do you want me to do?"

"I want you to—how does Alice say it?—suit yourself. If you want to spend time with Alice doing something you enjoy, go ahead. I know that would make her happy. But if you want to help your brother and me, we would love to have you."

Not expecting the choice to be hers, Cassie struggled with the decision. "I think I'll go help Alice for a while and then come out and help you," Cassie compromised with herself.

"Suit yourself," deadpanned Robby, getting an attitude look from his sister.

Cassie lost track of time and came back outside just as Jack and Robby were getting ready to clean up. She cleaned the brushes while Jack took down the ladders and Robby closed up the paint cans and put the scrapers away.

"What do you think, Robby, will I be done by Thursday?"

"I don't know," said Robby. "You won't work Monday morning, and you still have the porch and garage to do. And it could rain."

"You could have just said no," Cassie piped up. Robby thought about saying something back, but she had the hose.

"I've been saving the porch until last in case it does rain. I'd like to get done next week. I'm waiting for a call about a plumbing job that could happen soon."

"You've worked such long hours on this house that you haven't had time to check back on jobs you've applied for," said Robby. "Should you do that Monday too?"

"I've been doing pretty well with that," said Jack. "Alice lets me use her phone to make a few calls when I need to."

Just then Megan stuck her head out the back door. "Guys, come and see what Alice and I have been doing."

"Just a quick look, Megan," said Jack, "unless you don't mind waiting for dinner."

"I'm hungry now," said Robby.

"I'd hate to see your grocery bill," said Alice, getting a bag of potato chips out of the cupboard.

"I hate to see it myself," said Jack, watching Robby and Cassie both try to get a handful of chips at the same time.

"Look at all these pictures," said Megan. The kitchen table was covered with albums, boxes, and bundles of pictures bound with rubber bands. "We still have a lot of sorting to do." She went on seriously, "Alice said it's all right to do that on Sunday." Megan looked at her dad expectantly.

"Tomorrow?" asked Cassie.

"Yeah," said Megan.

"That would be up to Alice," said Jack. "If she wants to put up with you tomorrow, I will bring you over."

"Well, that's settled," said Alice. Megan and Cassie both grinned.

CHAPTER 19

Jack paced around the house nervously, trying not to wake up Sally. He had awakened at six, got the kids up and off to school, read the paper, and it still wasn't even eight thirty. He had called, just in case, but the recording said the office hours were nine to five. The night before, he had gathered up all the papers he thought he would need at the bank while he was waiting for Sally to come home.

After he filled her in on the rest of the day, she asked him, "Have you had a chance to talk to Robby?"

"No." Jack shook his head. "I haven't seen him in one of those moods since Friday. I was going to wait until he went into another funk to say something to him. There were a lot of other people around yesterday, and today he was at church in the morning, at a friend's in the afternoon, and at that youth meeting tonight. All of that probably took his mind off whatever is bothering him. I'm watching, though."

"Good."

"Oh, I forgot. He did talk to me when he came home tonight, and he seemed a little uneasy. The Sunday before they go on the work mission there will be a parents' meeting to explain how it works and to answer questions. I guess he thought I might not go."

Sally gave him a "go on" look. "Of course I'll go." Jack bristled. "Why wouldn't I?"

"Robby evidently wondered; did you reassure him?"

"What do you think?"

"I'm sure you did." She smiled.

"Then why did you ask?"

"Just to irritate you," teased Sally. "I don't get many chances to do that these days. And I miss it."

Jack chuckled. "So do I."

When the clock inched its way to two minutes past nine, Jack called the bank and got right through to Jeff. He explained what he wanted to do and told Jeff about his recent experience with "that old sourpuss," as Alice called him.

"I'm sorry, Jack," said Jeff. "I can't do much about that. He's been here a long time."

"Is he your boss?"

"No, but he thinks he's everybody's boss. He's not very popular," said Jeff. After a pause, he went on, "I didn't say that. I'm the new guy around here."

"So can you help me?" asked Jack.

"I can figure how much money you'll need, but I can't do the actual transaction with you."

"So I'll have to deal with him."

"Sorry. And you'll need to have the check certified."

It was past eleven, and Jack was trying to calm himself down on the way to the bank. Jeff had called him back with the numbers, he picked up Alice and took her to her bank to get the check, and now he had to deal with Sourpuss.

Jeff had assembled all the paperwork and put it on the unpleasant man's desk, so he was expecting them. But he made them wait fifteen minutes before he would see them. He gave them a cursory nod and motioned them toward some chairs. He then pretended to go over the papers, which Jack was sure he had already read.

He looked up. "Do you have the money, Mr. Wilson?" Jack handed him the check.

He checked the amount against Jeff's figures and said, "I'll see that this gets processed."

Realizing that they were being dismissed, Jack said, "Do I get something that states that my home is no longer in foreclosure?"

"That will come in the mail."

"When?"

"Two to three weeks."

Jack was about to explode, but Alice beat him to the punch. "I want a receipt for the check."

He looked at her patronizingly and said, "The check is certified."

"But how do we know you are?" she shot back.

Before he could respond to that, Alice stood up and turned to Jack. "See, I was right."

"About what?" asked Jack.

"He is an old sourpuss." And she marched out the door.

Jack got up and followed her. As he reached the door, he turned back with a barely suppressed smile on his face and said, "Thanks for your help and have a nice day."

Tuesday found Jack working on the porch. It was a warm day, but there was a light rain falling. He had gone home in a sour mood the evening before, unhappy with his progress because of what he thought of as a wasted morning. But it wasn't. A huge load had been lifted from his shoulders. His story about Alice and Sourpuss brought roars of laughter from his kids. His spirits lifted, he had enjoyed a rare evening of contentment.

Soon after lunch a little red car pulled in the driveway. A man got out and came up on the porch. "You must be Jack," he said pleasantly.

Jack looked him over. "I am."

The man walked over to him with his hand out. "I'm Scot."

Jack put his brush down and looked for a rag to wipe his hands on. Not finding one, he started wiping them on his shirt. "It'll come off." Scot smiled and shook his hand.

"Are you here to see Alice?" Jack asked. He was suspicious.

"Yeah, but I also wanted to meet you."

Jack picked up his paintbrush again, hoping to send a message. "Am I going to have to start calling you Sourpuss too?" Alice said through the screen door.

"Did you just happen to invite him over here today, Alice?"

"Nope, we pay him to figure things out for himself."

Jack looked at Scot. "I've been looking for a chance to stop over since you started," said Scot.

"So Don put you up to it." It wasn't a question.

"No. I asked him if he thought it was a good idea."

"What did he say?"

Scot hesitated. "He said something about wearing hockey gear."

Alice laughed and excused herself to go back to her soap opera. Scot walked over and sat on the porch rail and watched Jack paint. "I've enjoyed getting to know your family, so I thought I should take the opportunity to meet the dad," said Scot.

"Is that what Alice calls sneaking up on me?"

Scot was baffled. "I don't—"

"Never mind," Jack interrupted. "It was just some weird thing she said to me."

Scot decided not to pursue that. "Are you getting a lot of pressure from your family?"

"About church?"

"Yes."

"No."

"No squabbling about it?"

"None."

"Is it clear to you that it matters to them that you don't come?"

Jack let out a long sigh. "Yes."

"Are you getting any unwelcome pressure from anyone from the church?"

"Just Alice."

"Alice doesn't count."

Jack chuckled. "It's very obvious that that's not true."

"I just wanted to be sure that you haven't been offended by anyone from my congregation."

Jack looked at Scot. "All they've done is help me. How could I be offended by that?"

"Not even Don?"

"I've exchanged unpleasant words with Don twice. Both times I was the offender. But you already knew that."

"I've had one conversation with Don about you. He told me about the incident over the Heifer book. I asked him if he knew of anyone who was looking for some work, and he suggested you for this job."

"There had to be more to it than that. What about your theory about me and my parents?"

Jack felt himself tensing up.

"He just told me that you were dragged every Sunday to a church where the minister in a black robe leaned out over the pulpit, gripped it so tight that his knuckles turned white, and screamed that if you didn't stop sinning you were going to hell. I wouldn't go to a church like that. My church isn't like that. We talk about love and forgiveness and grace."

"So I've been told," Jack conceded.

"Was it like that every week?"

"It was like that every week, and it was like that at home." Jack's voice turned bitter.

"So home wasn't any fun either," said Scot.

"I stayed away as much as I could without getting in trouble, and then I didn't even care about that anymore. I moved out right after high school, and nobody cared."

"Are you sure?"

"Nothing was said." Jack's voice was almost sad.

"Well, here's my theory. Actually, it's not my theory; it's something I remember from a counseling class I took in seminary. As I remember the example, this young girl's father died, and she became angry when her mother began seeing someone. But instead of directing her anger toward her mother, she directed it at the boyfriend. As time went on, the situation worsened, causing conflict between the mother and daughter, but the girl never expressed the real source of her anger to her mother—that she missed her dad, that she felt abandoned, that she didn't want anyone to replace her father—so they never sat down and settled it." Scot paused, hoping for a response from Jack. He just kept painting.

"Am I saying this so it makes sense?" he asked. "Or are you even listening?"

"Keep talking."

"This is how I understood the professor's explanation. The girl was angry with her mother but didn't want to fight with her mother because she loved her mother, so she vented her anger at the boyfriend. She didn't love the boyfriend, so it didn't matter if she hurt him. Of course, she overlooked the fact that her mother was being indirectly hurt."

Scot waited. After a while Jack stopped painting and faced Scot. "So I'm the girl, my parents are the mom, and the church is the boyfriend?"

"The analogy is not perfect, but I'm guessing that you never had an honest discussion with your parents about how horrible the whole church experience was for you and that you felt robbed of a relationship with them because of the church. So you've harbored this hatred toward the church, which eliminates any possibility of reconciliation with your parents, because the church is part of their lives."

"So if I come to church that will solve everything?"

"Not at all," Scot answered. "Of course you need to come to church, but the overriding problem is that you are estranged from your parents and you have buried it deep in your subconscious."

"So you're telling me that the responsibility for getting things out in the open was the girl's, that the mother wasn't a part of the problem."

"Absolutely not. The point the professor was trying to make is that some people will choose to not fight with someone they love who has caused their anger and will deflect their anger to someone they don't have to love. You, however, have also chosen to avoid the ones you love altogether."

"So are you going to tell me what I should do?" asked Jack. *Here comes the pitch*, he thought.

"No. My first concern is for your family. I consider them to be a part of my church, and so I feel a responsibility to minister to them. They are unhappy because you won't come to church with them, so I am suggesting that you consider their feelings and think about checking out what is so appealing to them."

Jack didn't respond. It became clear to Scot that he wasn't going to. "Your situation with your parents is very complex, Jack. If you would ever decide to try to restore your—"

"You can't restore something that never existed," snapped Jack. "It was like I was an inconvenience. I don't think they ever intended to have children; it was just bad luck that they did—for everybody. I never did anything but eat, sleep, and chores at my home. I never had friends over because they didn't measure up to my parents' standards. What's to restore?"

I'll bet he's never told anyone but his wife that, thought Scot. "Did you do well in school?" he asked.

"I was an honor student."

"Did you get praise for that?"

"It was expected."

"Would you have gone to hell if you got bad grades?"

"I was never told that." Jack tried not to smile. "Maybe that was my reward."

"Was there ever any talk of college?"

"Not much. I wanted to be an engineer, but I had to get away. If I went to college, I would have still been under their control."

"Does Sally know all this?" asked Scot.

"Yes."

"Robby?"

"No."

"Given your situation growing up, do you realize what a remarkable job you have done raising your own children?"

"Sally and I are raising our children." Jack was emphatic.

"And you've all managed to keep loving each other through some very difficult times," observed Scot.

I can't get mad at this guy, thought Jack. *Three weeks ago I would have splattered paint on him and run him off the porch. Maybe it is sneaking up on me.* "I guess we have."

Scot pushed himself off the rail and went over to shake hands with Jack. "Thanks for the conversation, Jack. If you ever need anything you think I can help you with, you know where to find me. I'm going to stop in and chat with Alice."

How did he get me to tell him all that stuff? Jack asked himself. *Maybe I just wanted to tell somebody besides Sally. But why? Was it really as bad as I told him it was? Maybe Sally could make some sense of it.*

CHAPTER 20

"You seem to be in a good mood," said Don, as he and Robby settled in at Taco Bell. Robby had talked nonstop since Don picked him up at school.

"My dad got the mortgage straightened out, one more week of school, three weeks until the work mission, what's not to be happy about?"

"And you're going to have steady income." Don smiled.

"Yeah, I'm going to start next week. That should give me some spending money for the mission trip. My dad says I have to save some of it, though."

"Good advice."

"This is the last Wednesday for the after-school program," said Robby.

"How long have we been doing this?"

"Since February." Robby had an odd smile on his face.

"What?" asked Don.

"Nothing." Robby stifled a laugh.

Don narrowed his eyes and waited. "Have you heard of the book *Tuesdays with Morrie?*" Robby asked.

"Yes."

"Have you read it?"

"No, but Lucy has," said Don. "I sort of know the story."

"My mom's reading it, and I asked her what it was about." Robby was grinning again.

"I don't get the joke," said Don, having no idea what Robby thought was so funny.

"I've been thinking about this weird idea. I think you should write a book."

"Why? About what?"

"About all the stuff that's happened. You could call it *Wednesdays with Robby.*" Robby was pleased with himself.

"You are a strange child," said Don. "You worry yourself sick that you're going to be found out, and now you want a book written about it."

Robby turned serious. "I've also thought of another title."

"I'm not sure I want to hear it."

"*Robby the Robber,*" he said. "That'll probably be my new nickname."

Don took a deep breath. "If I was going to write a book about 'all this stuff'—which I'm not—I would title it *Robby Braveheart*, in honor of my brave friend." *Or better yet,* Robby's Torment, Don stopped short of saying.

"I sure don't feel brave. I'm so scared to tell my parents. I can't stop thinking about it. I'm not sure I can do it. I know you told me that none of these good things would have happened if I hadn't stolen the quarters, but that's what it was—stealing. I'm *not* brave." Robby buried his head in his hands.

"I did tell you that, Robby, but I've decided that's not exactly true. What you did was wrong, but that's not what got you connected to the church. Your remorse for doing it is what got you connected to the church. If you had taken the quarters and never felt remorse for doing it and just spent the money and went on with your life, that would have been the end of it. But being who you are, you didn't like yourself for doing it and you had the courage to undo what you had done wrong. Since then, things have fallen into place for your family in a big way. And I still believe that God had a hand in that."

Robby just sat there, slumped in the corner of the booth. "My mom and dad are so happy and relaxed since the foreclosure was dropped, and now I'm going to mess things up again."

Don's heart went out to his pathetic young friend. He had gone from being a normal, happy young man when Don picked him up to a self-convicted failure in a little over an hour. "Robby, I've told you before that your parents—"

"I know. I know what you're going to say; I just wish I could believe it."

Robby got up and refilled his Pepsi then slumped back down in the booth. Don decided to leave him alone. After a while, he said, "We better go get your sister."

Robby remained silent on the drive to the church. *What a contrast to the ride from school,* thought Don. *Maybe Jay can get him out of his funk.*

Jay was in a lengthy conversation on his cell phone, and they left without Robby talking to him. Cassie was her usual bubbly self, and if she noticed Robby's mood, she didn't say anything. Cassie said goodbye and was halfway up the drive before Robby go out of the van. Don gave him a look of understanding and said, "You can do it, dude. A lot of people are praying for you."

"I hope so," said Robby sadly and trudged off toward his house.

CHAPTER 21

Jack was feeling good about his progress. Yesterday had been a good day. He had finished everything that he would need extension ladders and the scaffold for. All he had left to do were the garage, a small area down low in the back, and part of the porch. He found himself anticipating the arrival of the men from church with some eagerness. He had decided that he would take the time to go with them to put everything back in the garage.

He laid the extension ladder on the ground and noticed an area near the foundation that Robby had missed when he was scraping. That sent his thoughts back to his conversation with his son the night before. His bedroom door was slightly open, and Jack could see his feet hanging over the end of the bed. He eased the door open and saw that Robby was lying face down, his face buried in his pillow.

"Everything okay?" Jack asked.

Startled, Robby raised up to see his dad standing there. "Yeah. I just felt a little sleepy."

"It's not like you to get sleepy at this time of night. You feel all right?"

"I'm okay, just a little worried about all the tests I have coming up." Which he was because he had been having trouble concentrating on his homework. He got up and went back over to his desk.

"Anything I can help you with?"

"No, it's mostly reading. I'm just not concentrating. Excited about the work mission I guess."

"You don't want to talk about it." Jack didn't like the sad look on his son's face. "You know you can—anytime."

"I know," said Robby, forcing a smile. "I'll work it out."

Jack got his scraper and cleaned the area off. He started to go back and start on the garage when two pickups came in the driveway. A car pulled up at the curb in front of the house. *Man, they brought the whole pack*, thought Jack.

They all shook his hand and then went around inspecting his work. "Is Alice satisfied?" asked Mike.

"If she's not, she hasn't said anything."

"She's satisfied," said Joe.

"It looks good, Jack," said Bob. "You do nice work."

They went right to work tearing down the scaffold and getting everything loaded in the trucks. Alice came out to watch them. She sat down in the porch chair, all dressed up with her purse in her lap. "Where are you going, fancy girl?" asked Butch.

"Sally's taking me shopping."

"You going to leave Jack here alone and unsupervised?" asked Ed.

"Well, he's sure not going with us." She snorted, getting the hoped-for reaction from all of them.

"Are you happy with your house?" asked Don.

"He'd never make a living painting. He's too particular."

"She's happy," said Joe.

Just then Sally drove up. Jack was prepared to introduce her to everyone but soon realized that they already knew her. She greeted them all by name and even gave Bob a hug. Jack just stood there feeling very much out of place. "Looks like you've got plenty of good help," she said to him.

"Well, there are a lot of them," said Alice as she came down the porch steps. "You boys have fun putting that stuff away; Sally and I have things to do."

"When do you expect to be back?" Jack asked Sally.

"Not before lunch." She smiled and gave him a kiss on the cheek.

As the women walked out to the car, Mike said to Jack, "Man, you've got a great family. I've never seen Alice so happy." That brought nods of agreement from everyone.

They went back to the church and put everything back in the garage. "Let's go have coffee," said Ed. "Are you going to join us this time?" he asked Jack.

"If he doesn't, we're going to load all that stuff back on his truck," said Bob.

"I get a break from Alice, and then I have to put up with this," Jack complained.

They went inside, down a long hall to a room next to the kitchen. Mike and Joe made the coffee, and Bob showed up with some cookies that he'd scrounged from somewhere. "Cookies can't hide from Bob," Don explained to Jack.

Jack mostly listened as the conversation went from sports to politics to the economy. "This area just isn't recovering as fast as other places in the country," said Mike.

"Are you having any luck at all?" Butch asked Jack.

"None. I've probably sent out sixty résumés and made I don't how many phone calls and haven't had one response. When a hundred people are applying for the same job, you don't have much of a chance."

"I was talking to a guy in our home owner's association last week, and he said he had to hire four people from over one hundred and sixty applications," said Ed. "He had his assistant go through them all and eliminate all those who obviously didn't have the qualifications they were looking for, and he was able to throw out only about forty. Now he has to go through all the rest and come up with a short list of twelve to interview. He said after a while they all start to look alike."

Scot walked in the room and helped himself to a cup of coffee and a cookie. "Keep going; I didn't mean to interrupt," he said.

"He's got two for his short list that are recommendations from people he knows," Ed went on. "He said he's hired a lot of good people in the past on tips from colleagues and friends who know what he's looking for."

"What company does he work for?" asked Scot.

"Solar Systems."

"I have an application in there," said Jack.

"There's his man," said Scot. "I'll bet they could use a frustrated engineer."

"You're an engineer?" asked Don. *Where did Scot get that from?*

"No," said Jack. "I would have been if I had gone to college, but I went right to work instead."

"I don't know what jobs they're trying to fill, but do you think it's something you could do?" asked Ed.

"It sounded like a lot of technical stuff, but I've learned technical stuff before. This really sounded interesting to me."

"I'll see John this weekend," said Ed. "I'll tell him about you. Who knows, maybe he'll dig your app out and give it a closer look."

"Thanks," said Jack, not really placing much hope that anything would come of it.

As if there was some signal, the group started to get up to leave. *I guess the meeting's over*, thought Jack. He threw his cup and napkin in the trash and started for the door.

"Got time for lunch?" Don asked him.

Taken by surprise, Jack tried to think of a good excuse not to go. He couldn't. "Sure," he said without much conviction.

They drove separately and met at a small, local diner. "It looks like things are under control for you for now," said Don.

"We've dodged a big bullet, but it could happen again if I don't get a job soon."

"Maybe Ed will get you a shot at that job."

"I'm not getting my hopes up on that," said Jack. "He can't tell the guy he really knows me."

"Stranger things have happened."

"Not to me." *If you only knew*, thought Don.

"When we talked in Alice's front yard, you were very negative about the church. How do you feel about it now?"

"The preacher put you up to this?"

"No. Why?"

"He stopped by for a visit Tuesday afternoon," said Jack.

"Really," said Don. He seemed genuinely surprised. "How did that go?"

"He just asked me a lot of questions about my parents and the whole church thing."

"Did you answer them?"

"Mostly. You'll probably hear all about it from him." Jack was starting to get cynical.

"My chances of hearing about it from Scot are about as good as they would be if you had talked to the wall. Did you think we had a conspiracy going here?"

"You guys are hard to figure out," Jack replied.

"I thought you would trust us by now."

"It's getting harder not to," said Jack, forcing a smile.

"Did you resolve anything?"

"He just said that maybe the real cause of my anger was my parents but I was directing it at the church because it's more convenient—or something like that."

"You need to get rid of your anger toward your parents because you never really confronted them with it, but now you can't because you've separated yourself from them. You settled for peaceful coexistence instead of resolving the problem once and for all, and it hasn't worked. So you're using the church as a substitute to unload your anger because you still need to get rid of it. That's how I understood it."

Jack got a puzzled look on his face. Don waited for him to speak. "You know, that almost makes sense. I know that I wasn't paying very close attention when Scot was talking to me because I was irritated because he was talking to me. I've been trying to understand it ever since. I think I've got it now. Thanks."

"So do you think you might be able to show the church some mercy now?" Don asked him.

Jack thought about that. "I think I still feel some legitimate anger toward the church for the way I was treated."

"Maybe if you could give our church a chance to show you our way—the love and forgiveness of God and Jesus—you would find it possible to forgive your parents' church for its mistakes."

"I can feel myself getting sucked in." Jack wasn't smiling.

"Let it happen; enjoy the ride. It's a great feeling." Don was smiling. Jack wasn't buying it.

"There's more to it than the way you were treated, isn't there?" Don asked him.

Jack's face said yes. *Well now*, thought Don, *why didn't I figure this out before?* "Are you going to tell me what it is?"

Why should I, thought Jack. *You're going to have all the answers; just like those guys at work. Why not?* he decided. "I think I learned more about Christianity by listening to the three guys at the table next to me in the lunchroom at work than I did at church. Every day they would huddle together and read from the Bible and then talk about it."

"Did you ever join in or ask questions?" asked Don.

"Some guys tried, but they were pretty much ignored. They made it clear that they thought they were better than the rest of us."

"What did you learn about the Bible from listening to them—the story itself?"

"They talked a lot about the second coming and the end times and who was and wasn't going to hell. I'd heard a lot of that stuff before," Jack said.

"What about Jesus and his message?"

"That Jesus was the Son of God and he let him be crucified and he came back to life and … " Jack shrugged.

"And what?"

Jack had clearly become uncomfortable. "Look, it just doesn't make sense to me. I don't know what to say to my kids when they talk about stuff they heard at church. This whole praying thing—it just doesn't make sense. Why would God, if he had all this power, stick his son in the middle of all this mess and then let someone kill him? Everyone I've met from that church has been nice to me and my family. I've never met nicer people, but I don't want to sit around talking about stuff like that with them."

Don didn't know where to start. How could Jack have been exposed to two misguided sides of the Christian faith and never have been exposed to the very best part of it—the real heart of it? *From mean-spirited people to self-absorbed people who exclude the rest of the world and finally to us, who he wants to keep at arm's length because of those other people.*

"So you do believe that there is a God? An all-powerful God?"

"Yeah, I guess." Don's face told Jack that wasn't good enough. "Okay, I do. Yes."

"Describe him to me." Jack just shook his head. He didn't want to play. "Humor me," said Don.

"God created the universe, including people. He wrote out a set of rules on some rocks, which we pretty much ignore. And he's supposed to care about everyone, but that doesn't seem to be working out too well either." Jack's manner was somewhat condescending.

"What about Jesus?"

"Jesus—I don't know. He was a teacher. They say he could heal people. He was dead and then he wasn't. I just don't get it. Sounds like science-fiction to me." Jack's tone was softer.

"I'm going to try to help you with your understanding of God sending his Son to live among the people with powers to heal and who was a great teacher. There's a lot more to it than that, but this is a very important part. I'm going to try to explain it to you by telling you a story I heard about thirty years ago. I was coming back from a job late in the day when I got caught in a huge snowstorm. I was fifty miles from home and traveling about twenty miles an hour. I was listening to a Christmas program on the radio, and they played a tape of this Christmas story. I have never forgotten it. It calmed me down and took a lot of the stress out of my situation. Will you listen?"

Jack sighed. *I've been rude to this man twice already*, Jack told himself. *Am I going to regret this?* "Okay."

This is a story about a young family with a mother, a father, a ten-year-old girl, and an eight-year-old boy. They lived in a comfortable house on an acre of land at the edge of a small town. There was a small barn out back where they kept a pony. They were a very loving, happy family except for one thing. Church.

The mother and the two children went to church every Sunday and took part in other activities during the week. The father, however, would not go with them. He simply did not believe the story of Jesus. "It makes no sense to me," he told them. As the children got older, they were more and more bothered by that.

It was Christmas Eve, and they were getting ready to go to their traditional candlelight service. It was the children's favorite service of the year. Just as they were leaving, the girl hugged her father and said sadly, "I wish you would go with us just once, Daddy. It's so beautiful with all the candles and the flowers."

He kissed her on the forehead, told them all to have a nice time, and walked them to the door. As they were driving away, he noticed a few snow flurries in the air. A snowstorm had been predicted for later in the night, and he hoped it wasn't coming through early.

He closed the door, picked up his book, and settled himself

in his easy chair for a relaxed evening of reading. About twenty minutes later, he thought he heard a bump against the house. A few minutes later, he heard it twice more. He got up and looked out the big front window and saw that it had been snowing and it was starting to cover the ground. But he saw nothing that would cause the noises.

He sat back down in his chair, and before he could get his book open, he heard it again, only louder. And then there were more. *Are those kids across the road out throwing snowballs?* he wondered. He went and opened the door and was greeted with a gust of wind that blew snow into the house. It was snowing much harder now. He heard the thuds again and saw that it was birds hitting his front window. Then they started coming in bunches, a whole flock, hitting his window and dropping to the ground.

Then he noticed that none of them were flying off again. *Their wings are iced up! They can't take off! They're attracted by the light from the window, looking for shelter.* He also noticed that the snow had become wetter. The birds were flopping around on the ground, trying to shake off the ice. He turned off his living room light so whatever birds might still be coming wouldn't hit the window. He couldn't tell if any of them were actually injured.

He went back inside and put on his coat and boots. He wondered if he could just pick them up and brush the ice off their wings. They became more frantic than ever when he got near them. Then he had another idea. He went out to the barn, opened the door, and turned on the light. If they're attracted to light, he reasoned, maybe they can work their way back to the barn and thaw out in there. They just continued to flop around out of fear and desperation.

Determined to help them, he went back to the barn to get a snow shovel. He scraped a path about four feet wide toward the barn. After he'd gone about fifteen feet he was out of breath. He went another ten feet and then thought of something else. He went back to the barn and got some birdseed and sprinkled it along the area he had shoveled. He even threw some in among the birds. Same results.

The snow had eased up, but it had accumulated to almost two inches, making it difficult for the birds to get their wings high enough above the snow to flap their wings without getting more snow on them. His frustration increasing, he went on the other side of the birds and tried to shoo them toward the path he had shoveled. "Come on, you guys. Why don't you cooperate? I'm trying to help you."

Beside himself with frustration, he paced around the perimeter of the flock, unable to think of anything else he could do. "Why don't you get it!" he shouted. "I'm doing all these things for you, and you're not paying any attention."

Cold and soaked with sweat, he stood there in total despair. "If I could only change into a bird for a few minutes, I could tell them that I want to help them. I could make them understand what I'm trying to do."

In the distance he heard the church bell ring midnight. It was Christmas Day. He thought about what he had just said, and suddenly it was clear to him. Now he knew. Of course, that was why God came to earth in the form of a man. So he could talk to them. So he could make them understand.

He slumped to his knees in the snow. He stayed there with his head bowed. After a while, he became aware that the noise of the struggling birds had taken on a different sound. He looked up and saw that some of them were able to free their wings of the ice. It had warmed up just enough for the ice to start melting.

He watched them shake free and fly away, one by one. When the last one had gone, he got up, took his shovel back to the barn, patted the pony on the nose, turned out the light, closed the barn door, turned on the porch light, and sat on his front step and waited for his family to come home so he could tell them the good news.

Jack had listened politely to Don's story without interruption or any body language that would show approval or disapproval. He stared across the diner, deep in thought. Don didn't think that Jack had been listening intently, but he had listened. Finally Jack turned to Don and said, "That was an interesting story. Long, but interesting."

"But not convincing."

"I need to think about it some more. I need to run it past Sally."

Perfect, thought Don. *Maybe she can get him to open up about it.*

"While you're thinking about all that, give some consideration to the fact that a lot of the good things happening to you are because of your family's connection to the church."

"I don't need that pointed out to me." Jack was a little testy. *Be careful*, Don told himself.

"I didn't mean to sound patronizing; I was just trying to explain to you that we believe that God does his good works through people; that all goodness comes from God. I didn't mean to say that the church should get the credit."

Now what is he getting at? Jack wondered. He decided not to ask. He was ready to leave.

"Let me try again," said Don. "I'm not saying what I want to say." He paused to collect his thoughts. "We, the church, all of us believe that God has plopped your family in our midst so we can help you. Part of our faith covenant is that we will help people who need it. If we don't do that, shame on us; we have damaged our covenant with God. Jesus talked a lot about servanthood; this is what he meant."

Jack stood up, signaling the end of the conversation. "Thanks for listening," said Don, as they walked to their cars.

"I'm getting better at that too," said Jack. *Maybe it is sneaking up on me*, he thought. They shook hands and went their separate ways.

CHAPTER 22

Jack and Robby arrived at Alice's on Saturday before the other mission team members, Ben and Chelsea, showed up. Jack wanted to get the garage opened up and have things organized before they got there. He had made good progress on Friday and had hopes of finishing everything on Saturday. He got the feeling from Alice at lunch that she would like his help with the garage project. "I don't know if I can keep track of those young people," she had said. "They run around in circles like a bunch of ants on a cookie crumb." So he decided to take a day off from painting to help her. To his surprise, the idea had been a big hit with Robby.

"I want that stuff put in four piles," Alice had told him. "One for stuff I want to keep, one for stuff to go to Goodwill, one for trash, and an 'I haven't decided yet' pile."

Robby and Jack had just started pulling things out of the garage when Ben showed up. Robby introduced Ben to his dad and was going to explain the plan to him when Chelsea came walking up the driveway. He introduced her to Jack and then showed them both what they were going to do.

Alice sat in a lawn chair next to the driveway and passed judgment on the things they brought to her. They would then deposit them in the designated pile. The process was slowed down because many of the things had stories to go along with them and Alice would not send them to a pile until the story was told. But they enjoyed the stories and were disappointed when they would bring her something and she would just wave it off to one pile or another with barely a comment.

About a third of the way through the garage, Jack spied the nose of the lawnmower. He uncovered it and pushed it out beside his truck. He checked the gas tank and saw that it was dry. *A project for next week,* he decided. He looked at his watch. *Almost noon. These kids are going to want to eat soon.* He started to lift the mower into the truck when a voice stopped him. "Let me help you with that." He turned and saw a young man walking toward him.

"You must be Robby's dad," he said, offering to shake hands. "I'm Jay."

The famous Jay. *Am I going to have to listen to a lecture from him too?* Jack wondered. Jack shook his hand. "I'm Jack."

"If you don't have anything to do in two weeks, we have room for one more adult on the work mission."

So much for feeling each other out, thought Jack. "I don't think I'd fit in very well," he said, dismissing the idea.

"Robby says you can do anything. You could help the kids learn how to do things. Alice tells me you're running this project for her today."

"I don't know anybody, and they don't know me," said Jack. *Why does Robby like this guy? This is worse than the lectures.*

Jay gave him a crooked smile. "That could present a problem if anyone offers you a job. If you change your mind, just show up with your gear that Saturday morning," he said and turned to go to talk to Alice.

Jack stared after him. "You're not going to help me with this lawnmower?"

Jay stopped and turned around. "It's not that heavy, is it?" said Jay, looking foolish. He walked back and helped Jack lift it into the truck. "Don't tell Alice about this—or the kids."

Jack walked back over to the garage and was met by Robby. "Dad, we're hungry."

"Is it ten o'clock already?"

"Funny," said Ben.

Alice and Jack had not discussed the issue of lunch, and he assumed she was taking care of it. "I'm going to get pizza for everyone," Jay announced. "There's money in the budget for it."

"I'll decide what budget it comes from," said Alice. "You get those youngsters what they want."

Jack was waiting to see what Jay's response to that would be. Jay turned to Robby, Ben, and Chelsea and said in mock seriousness, "The queen mother has spoken. What can I get for you youngsters?" Even Alice had to laugh.

Jay called the order in on his cell phone and then left to pick up the pizza. Jack and the teenagers continued to bring things out of the garage.

"That boy is going to be a good preacher some day," said Alice.

"What do you mean?" asked Ben.

"I mean a real preacher. Go to seminary, get ordained, and get a church of his own."

"I thought he was a minister," said Robby.

"No." Ben shook his head. "He was an engineer. The youth program was in bad shape and needed a strong leader. He decided that God was calling him to do it, so he quit his job. Lucky for us."

Lucky for me, thought Robby, thinking of all the reassuring advice Jay had given him. And all the times he had just listened to him. Jack was listening to all this with interest as well. *There must be something to him to get an endorsement like that from Alice. Maybe he just takes a little more knowing.*

Jay soon came back with the pizza and some two-liter bottles of soda. Jack watched his son interact with his friends and Jay. *This is really good for him*, he admitted to himself. *This is what Sally is trying to tell me.* Jack noticed that Alice was also doing a lot of observing. She seemed to be taking pleasure in just listening to the young people enjoying one another's company.

"Robby, I'm sure glad you had the idea to get more help," said Alice. "You and I would've never been able to do this by ourselves. Did you pick these two?"

"Don't blame me; it's Jay's fault." Robby grinned. Chelsea threw a piece of pizza crust at him.

"Well, they're hard workers," Alice said to Jay. "If the rest of your group works this hard, they'll make our church proud when you go on your trip."

"All of our kids are good workers, Alice," said Jay. "All of them are going because they want to help someone else. But it's not just work; they have a lot of fun. Just like they're working for you but having fun as well."

"Is that your fault too?" asked Alice.

Jay laughed. "I'd like to take credit for it, but their parents are mostly to blame. You know all their parents; are you surprised?"

"Guess not," Alice admitted.

Soon after lunch Jay left. Before he did, he caught Jack as he was taking something Alice wanted to keep into the house. "I hope I didn't come on too strong before. I thought I knew enough about you to make that offer.

"It took me off guard. What made you think you knew enough about me?"

Jay shrugged. "I've heard things about you from four people I respect, and all of it's good. I guess you got a little testy with Don and Scot, but who wouldn't?"

"You haven't heard anything bad from Robby?"

"Robby has shared a lot of things with me. When I talk to any of these kids in confidence, I make sure their trust is not misplaced. But you can be sure your son loves and respects you and fully understands that you're going through a hard time. I consider it a privilege to have him in our group. Everyone likes him. He's made out of tough stuff. He's where he belongs."

It was close to four o'clock when Jack noticed that Alice was getting tired. She had stayed behind after lunch to rest for a while, but it had been a big day for her. "Alice, I think we should call it a day," Jack said to her, not sure how she would react.

"I'm tired, but what are we going to do with all this stuff spread all over the place?"

"We can put the throw-away pile at the curb; I see some people are already doing that," said Robby.

"We can take the things she wants to keep in the house," suggested Chelsea. "There's not that much of it."

Jack decided to stay out of it and let them work it out. Ben walked over to the garage. "Robby," he said, "we could put the other two piles on opposite sides of the garage and still have room to get the other stuff out."

Robby looked at the piles and then into the garage. "That'll work."

"Good idea," said Chelsea.

"Well, they don't need you, Jack." Alice laughed, getting out of her chair. "You might as well come inside with me and get some rest." Ben, much to her delight, walked over and gave her a high-five.

"Okay, all you smart guys, what about that little bit of stuff you haven't sorted through?" Jack said smugly. "What are you going to do about that?"

They looked at each other. "Can you guys come over after school Monday?" asked Chelsea.

"I can," said Robby. Ben nodded yes.

"Good, I'll see you Monday," said Alice as she walked to the house. She stopped at the door and turned around. "But I'll see you in church tomorrow first," she added, sneaking a sidelong glance at Jack.

CHAPTER 23

Jack couldn't have been in a fouler mood. He set his wet shoes on the rug just inside the back door, dropped his soggy socks beside them, and walked barefoot through the house to change into some dry clothes. Yesterday, Monday, he had been able to finish the porch in spite of the on-and-off rain. Robby and his friends also ignored the rain and showed up to finish sorting out Alice's garage. They waited until it stopped raining long enough for Alice to get inside the garage and were able to do it without putting anything outside, except the throwaways, which they took to the curb in between showers. Alice was even able to go back through the "I haven't decided yet" pile, so all that was left in the garage was the Goodwill pile.

"One of those fellows from church will take that away for me when he gets a chance," said Alice.

"My dad could take it," said Robby. "We could load it right now if it wasn't raining."

"Let's do it Saturday," said Ben. "It won't take that long."

"Don't you think you should ask Jack before you make all these plans?" asked Alice.

"I'll go ask him," said Chelsea. "When it stops raining," she added, looking out through the garage door.

But just then Jack came running around the side of the house with his paint can and brush. "It's raining harder than I thought," he said, shaking off what water he could.

Chelsea asked him about Saturday. "The only thing that might get in the way is that plumbing job I've been waiting to hear about. But let's plan on it."

That was yesterday. Today started out partly cloudy and went downhill from there. Jack had only the garage to finish and would have made it except for a sudden downpour right after lunch. By the time he could get everything put away, he was soaked. That was frustrating enough, but the overriding problem contributing to his mood was that he hadn't heard about the plumbing job.

They would have enough money to comfortably make their June house payment when he got his final check from Alice, but they were already three days into the grace period, and he had made it a goal to avoid that. So much for goals. He also wanted to get a jump-start on the July payment, which was why he was anxious about the plumbing job. He was determined not to get behind again. He finished dressing, gathered up his wet clothes to throw in the laundry, and went to unpack what was left in his cooler. Then his cell phone rang.

Robby got to the church just before the storm hit. He had finished his last exam early and thought he would stop by and see Jay. He wanted to know how much he still owed for the mission trip after getting credit for the garage project. Jay's office was down a long hall past the minister's office. Robby glanced in and saw Pastor Scot hunched over his computer. A few steps later, he heard, "He's not here, Robby."

Robby stopped and went back. "Jay just left for some meeting," said Scot. "Anything I can do for you?"

"No, I'm just curious how much I still owe for the mission."

"Can't help you with that. Will Alice's garage cleanup get you close?"

"I hope so. Depends on how much she paid us."

"Alice was very pleased with the job you guys did. I have a feeling that just having people around was more important than getting her garage cleaned out," said Scot.

"We all had fun. Ben said it was a lot like being on the mission."

"We're all glad you're going. Bring back some good stories."

Robby left a little disappointed but thought he could try again tomorrow. He liked talking to Jay. He always gave him positive advice about his dilemma. Robby wondered, not for the first time, what Pastor Scot would have to say if he knew. All the activity of the weekend, and even yesterday, had kept Robby's mind off his problem. Now it was creeping back into his thoughts again. He had decided to wait until after the parents' meeting on Sunday to tell his parents.

Nearing his house, Robby saw his dad's truck in the driveway. *I'll bet he got rained out; that won't put him in a good mood. I'm not in the best of moods myself,* he thought as he went in the back door. Robby unslung his backpack, put it on the table, and headed for the refrigerator. He noticed Jack's boots and socks on the rug. He took a long pull out of the milk carton and fished some lunch meat out of the package. He heard his dad's voice and figured out that he was talking on the phone.

"Yes … yes. No, that's not a problem. Nine o'clock. I'll be there. Thank you." Robby listened to Jack's end of the conversation. *Finally, the call about the plumbing job,* he thought. Robby took another gulp of milk and put the carton back. He went into the living room and saw his dad sitting on the couch with a look of disbelief on his face.

"Was that about the plumbing job?" asked Robby, not sure anymore that it was.

"No." Jack's voice sounded vacant.

"What, then?" Robby asked anxiously.

Jack opened his mouth to speak and then closed it again. A few seconds later he said, in the same voice, "I have a job interview."

It was Robby's turn to struggle for words. "Tomorrow at nine o'clock." Jack answered Robby's questions, his voice sounding more natural now. "That guy Ed knows, he actually called me." Jack was talking more to himself.

"I'm lost." Robby finally got some words out.

Jack told Robby about Ed saying he would call someone he knew where Jack had put in an application. "Awesome!" said Robby.

"I sent out all those résumés, made all those phone calls, and didn't get one call back. Then somebody I know makes a call to someone he knows, and I get an interview."

"And someone you just met," observed Robby. He wanted to say "someone from church."

The back door opened, followed by Cassie's voice, "We're home!" She and Megan came into the living room, trailing their book bags behind them. They were stopped short by the odd look on the faces of their father and brother. "What happened?" asked Cassie.

"Nothing bad," said Jack, breaking into a big grin.

"Something good," said Robby, enjoying his sisters' bewilderment.

"Come on!" said Cassie.

Jack motioned for Robby to tell them. "Dad has a job interview tomorrow."

Cassie covered her mouth with her hands. "Will you have a job then?" asked Megan, running over to her father.

"Maybe," said Jack. "They are going to talk to some other people and then hire the four they think are the best."

"I want to see Mom's face when you tell her," said Robby.

"She doesn't get off until ten."

"We could take a nap after dinner, and you could wake us up when she gets home," said Cassie.

Before Jack could say no, Robby made his pitch. "Dad, tomorrow is the last day of school; all I have is one test, and they're just going to do fun stuff. What will it hurt if we stay up? We're all too excited to sleep anyway." His sisters gave him a chorus of support.

Jack thought it over. He was too excited to argue with them. "Okay," he said, "but there better not be any grumbling about being tired in the morning. Robby, have you studied enough for that test?"

"I will," he promised. "Who gets to tell Mom?"

"Can I do it, please, please, please?" begged Megan, jumping up and down and clapping her hands.

"I know," said Cassie. "Let's all tell her together."

"I like it," said Robby.

"Okay," said Megan.

I've completely lost control, thought Jack.

They did their chores, had dinner, watched a little TV, and were all playing a board game on the floor when Sally came home. She walked into the living room and couldn't believe what she saw. "Hi, Mom," they all said.

"Is someone going to explain this to me?" She looked at Jack.

Robby, Cassie, and Megan got up and stood side by side in a row. "Your children have a little announcement for you." Jack grinned.

"Dad has a job interview tomorrow," they said in unison.

Sally was caught completely off guard. She just stood there with her mouth open. "They wanted to see your reaction, so I let them stay up."

"Oh, Jack," said Sally. They locked their arms around each other in a long embrace. Sally kissed him warmly.

"Eeew," said Cassie.

"I don't need to see this," said Robby. Megan just giggled.

Sally stuck her tongue out at them and kissed Jack again, getting another round of good-natured disapproval from her children.

"Okay, off to bed," said Jack. They all gave quick hugs and went to their rooms like they had promised.

Jack told Sally all the details about the phone call. He also confessed to her how nervous he was. "I've never interviewed for a job before."

"Didn't they talk about that at some of those job seminars you went to?" asked Sally.

"Almost all of them," said Jack. "I saved some of those handouts; I think I'll read through them again."

"You also need to call Ed and thank him for his help."

Jack shook his head. "I'm going to thank him in person. I'll stop at the church Thursday and talk to him." *And while you're there, hang out with your new buddies.* Sally smiled to herself.

CHAPTER 24

Jack fidgeted nervously in a chair across from the reception desk. He had misjudged how long it would take him to get to Solar Systems and was in their parking lot twenty minutes before his appointment. His plan was to arrive ten minutes early. He read over some of the interviewing notes again and then went inside.

Jack had awakened at six, took a shower, ate, and was ready to go by seven. Then the kids got up, and he occupied himself by helping them get off to school. They all gave him a hug and wished him good luck. By eight he was a nervous wreck. *Why did I drink that coffee?* he scolded himself. He reread the handouts about interviewing but wasn't really concentrating.

He heard Sally stirring and went to tell her he was leaving. "I'm sorry," she said sleepily. "Why didn't you wake me?"

"You don't get enough sleep as it is. Besides, I probably wouldn't be very good company."

"You'll be fine," she reassured him. "I know you'll do well."

But he wasn't fine. His mouth was dry, and his palms were sweaty. *I can't shake hands with sweaty palms*, he groaned to himself. He tried to casually dry them on his pants. The clock inched to five minutes past the hour. The receptionist gave him an apologetic smile.

Then a man came through the door and walked toward Jack with his hand out. "Jack, come on back. I'm John. Sorry to keep you waiting; some people just don't know how to say good-bye."

They shook hands, and Jack followed him down a short hall into his office. John motioned him into a chair in front of his desk. John sat down and picked up Jack's application. He sort of waved it at him and said, "You've only ever had one job."

Jack didn't know what to say. He didn't even know if it was a question "Well, except for flipping burgers while you were in high school," John added, looking at the application again. "Did you ever look for another job in all that time?"

"No."

"Ever think about it?"

"No." *What's he trying to find out?*

"Looks like you were doing some pretty high-tech stuff."

"I always wanted to be an engineer," said Jack, surprised at himself. *Why did I say that?*

"Why didn't you?"

Jack thought how to phrase it. "It didn't work out for me to go to college."

"Tell me about your family."

The abrupt change of subject only added to Jack's uneasiness. "Isn't it on the application?"

"Just names and ages."

"My wife dropped out of college to be a stay-at-home mom. She still very much wants to be a teacher. She was going to enroll in college last fall, but I got laid off. Now she's working two part-time jobs."

"And that bothers you?" John interrupted.

"Very much." John waited for him to continue. "I have three children who are my pride and joy—a freshman in high school son who is mature beyond his years most of the time, a sixth-grade daughter aged eight through fifteen, depending on the day, or moment, and a second-grade daughter who lights up the room."

John smiled. "Ed told me you had a great family."

"If it wasn't for Ed, I probably wouldn't be here."

"No, you wouldn't. I found your application buried in a pile where it didn't belong. We get so many it's hard not to miss some we should really look at. Yours should not have been missed."

Jack just shrugged, and then he had a thought. "Can I add another reference to my application?"

"I don't know why not." Jack gave him Don's name.

"Here's how this is going to work," John told him. "I've picked out twelve applicants to interview. I want to narrow that to eight by Friday and then schedule second interviews for next week and settle on four. I don't make promises or guarantees to anyone, but I need to know if there are any days you're not available next week."

Back in his truck Jack was trying to reconstruct the interview. It seemed as though John wasn't impressed one minute and then was ready to hire him the next. He didn't know what to think. Maybe Sally could make some sense of it.

"You were only in there fifteen minutes?" Sally couldn't believe it.

"If that." Jack shrugged.

"What did he ask you?"

Jack recited the whole interview to her, leaving out the part about him being bothered because she worked two jobs. He didn't want to have that conversation again.

"So first he acts unimpressed by your work history, then he asks about your family, then all but tells you he's going to bring you back for a second interview."

"Plus he made that remark about me doing high-tech stuff."

"You put on the application that you were a tool and die maker?" asked Sally.

"I think that's what he was talking about."

"I think it was an odd interview, but I think you should be optimistic." Jack's optimism started to take a nosedive Friday afternoon. He started getting anxious around midmorning but convinced himself that it was still too early to start worrying. By noon that argument didn't work anymore. The kids started coming home around three and didn't need to be told that their dad wasn't in the best of moods. Jack banged around in the kitchen fixing dinner, and no one was brave enough to try to help him.

"I'm sorry, you guys," Jack said as they sat down to dinner. "I guess I shouldn't have gotten my hopes up."

"We're sorry too, Daddy," said Megan.

"Maybe he'll call tomorrow," said Robby, knowing that it was unlikely.

Cassie just picked at her food.

Sally, on the other hand, became highly agitated when she heard the news. "I can't believe he led you on like that and then didn't call you back."

"He said he doesn't make promises or guarantees."

"I think you should call him." Jack just looked at her. "Monday morning. You deserve an explanation."

"I'll think about it."

The disappointment spread through the whole family. The girls lay around in front of the TV Saturday morning, only half-watching, and Sally was uncharacteristically somber. Jack and Robby went to meet Ben and Chelsea at Alice's.

After they had been there about a half hour, Alice said to Robby, "Did your dad get up on the wrong side of the bed this morning?" Robby explained what was going on.

"Guess I don't blame him."

By the time they finished loading his truck Jack's spirit had lifted a little. Jack, Ben, and Robby squeezed into the cab of the truck and went to the Goodwill drop-off. Chelsea stayed back to help Alice rearrange some things in her house. Jack listened to Ben and Robby talk about the work mission and found himself wondering about Jay's offer.

Jack and Robby got back home at lunchtime. There was a note from the girls that they were at a friend's. By the time lunch was over, Jack's bad mood was back. Desperate for something to do to take his mind off his problems, Jack started tinkering with Alice's lawnmower. After a few minutes he went back inside, where Robby was slouched in front of the TV. "Let's see if we can get Alice's lawnmower running. If you're going to use it, you should learn how to take care of it." Robby put on his shoes and followed his dad outside.

Jack showed him how to drain the oil. What there was of it was mostly sludge. "That should be drained every year before you put it away for the winter." Next he had Robby remove the spark plug and clean it and did the same for the air filter. They replaced the oil, put in some gas, and tried to start the mower.

"Take the spark plug out again, and we'll go get a new one," said Jack after several futile attempts.

They put in the new plug, and on Robby's second pull, the motor sputtered to life, belching out clouds of foul smoke. They stood back and let the mower run for a while. "Shut it off, and start it again," said Jack. This time there was a lot less smoke and it ran a lot smoother.

Jack explained to Robby the importance of keeping grass from building up on the underside of the mower and showed him how to sharpen the blade. By the time he was finished cleaning it all up Robby thought the mower looked almost new. *All I ever did before was put gas in it, start it, and push it. Now I pretty much know how it works.*

They had spent several hours working together with almost no conversation, and yet Robby had never felt such a closeness with his dad. He had noticed some of that when they were painting, but there was almost always someone else around. Would it be like that after next week? Would his dad even want to talk to him? He knew he would but was sure it would never be the same.

Don ended the Sunday school lesson early. "I want to talk to you about the work mission. You may hear some of this again from Jay. Some of you will be going for the first time. Try to understand how important it is to the community you're going to that you are simply there to help them. No matter how much you get done or don't get done, just your presence will mean something to them.

"It is also important for them to tell their stories. They have a need to tell someone what they have gone through, especially the older folks. It's okay to put down your hammer or your paintbrush or lean on your shovel or rake and give them your attention.

"Maybe the hardest thing you'll have to deal with is the job you are given. I'm sure you're all fired up to put on a new roof, build a handicap ramp, put up drywall, or any number of 'important' jobs. But you might end up cleaning up a mosquito-infested creek bed or clearing weeds in a vacant lot with no one around to even know that you're there. It may not seem important, but it is. Humble yourselves and do it cheerfully.

"Most importantly, conduct yourselves at all times in a way that people will see that God is working in your life; that you are there as God's servant, helping God's people.

"That's my lecture for today. Bring back a lot of good stories."

Robby hung back and helped Don straighten up the room. He told him about the interview.

"That had to be disappointing," said Don sympathetically.

"I'm not sure my dad is in the right mood to come to the parents' meeting this afternoon."

"Do you want to tell him not to come?"

"No, I want him to come, but I'm afraid someone will say something that he'll take the wrong way."

"Your dad has gotten over a lot of that, Robby; I think you should trust him." *More of Robby's torment*, thought Don.

On the way home, Sally noticed that Robby wasn't his usual upbeat self after church. "You're awfully quiet," she said to him.

"What's going on?"

"I'm kind of worried about the parents' meeting."

"Why?"

"What if Dad gets mad about something?"

"If you're really concerned, I'll say something to him."

"No!" said Robby. "I don't want him to know I'm worried."

Sally smiled at him. "Robby, I really don't think you need to worry. Your dad has become quite comfortable around those people." Robby was still worried.

They got to the church a few minutes early, but it looked as though almost everyone was already there. People were standing around in clusters, in no hurry to sit down. Ben waved Robby over, and somebody's mother latched on to Sally. Before Jack could feel out of place, Mike walked over to him.

"Hi, Jack, glad you could come." They shook hands, and Mike started introducing him to people. Then Jay spied him.

"Are you ready to sign on?"

"You might go?" Mike was excited.

Jack wanted to be somewhere else. The truth was he had given it some thought until the interview came up. "I might have a chance for a job," said Jack.

"I heard you had an interview," said Mike. "Still waiting to hear back?"

"Still waiting."

"I hope you get the job," said Jay, "but if you don't the offer is still open."

"If he goes, I want him," said Mike.

A boy and a girl ran up to Jay, talking at the same time, making it impossible to understand either one of them. That ended the uncomfortable situation for Jack. He looked around for Sally, but before he could go over to her, he was approached by a blond woman.

"Hi, you must be Robby's dad. I'm Joanie, Ben's mother."

"Hello, I'm Jack."

"Ben said he had a good time working at Alice's. I think he and Robby are becoming good friends."

"They all worked hard that day," said Jack. "Ben would be a good friend for Robby to have."

"Thanks." Joanie smiled. "We're glad to have your family in our church. I've particularly enjoyed Megan."

Before Jack had a chance to respond to that, Jay called for everyone to sit down so he could start the meeting. *That's twice I've been lucky,* he thought. He found Sally, and they sat near the back of the room.

Jay handed out itineraries for the trip and explained what kind of work they might be doing. "We won't know for sure until we get there, of course." He went over the rules of conduct that they had all agreed to when they registered for the trip.

"He's got everything covered," Jack whispered to Sally.

Jay opened up the floor for questions, and several hands went up. He answered them all to everyone's satisfaction and then closed the meeting with a prayer. Jack looked at his watch. *Just a little over an hour, not bad.* He and Sally got up to leave, and he noticed that almost everybody was back in groups talking just like they were before the meeting. No one was in a hurry to leave. He said something to Sally.

"That's the way it is after church too," she said.

"Do you know Ben's mother?" asked Jack.

"Pastor Joanie?"

"She's a minister?" Jack had no idea.

"She's the children's minister. Have you never heard Megan say how much she likes Pastor Joanie?" Jack knew he deserved the rebuke.

People were slowly leaving now, so Sally and Jack went over to pry Robby away from a group of his friends. Ben and Chelsea greeted them as they walked up, and Robby introduced the others. Jack was pleased to see how well accepted his son was in this group. *Were there churches like this when I was his age?* Jack wondered.

"There's a rumor that you might go with us next week," Ben said to Jack.

Jack narrowed his eyes. "Jay invited me to go, but I haven't really considered it," he said carefully, wondering why Jay would lead them to believe that.

"Any chance?" asked Ben.

"I have to be available in case I get any calls about a job. I can't take the chance being gone that long."

"If you miss a call, they will go right on to someone else. It wouldn't be worth the risk." Sally came to his rescue.

"But I hope you all have a good time; I know Robby is looking forward to it," said Jack, starting to move away toward the door. Nobody pursued it any further, so they eased out of the room and down the hall.

Robby caught up with them in the parking lot. "You didn't tell me Jay asked you to go." He was a little testy.

"I should have," Jack confessed. "I didn't think he would tell anyone."

"He didn't. Mike said something about it to us." *Thanks, Mike,* Jack said to himself.

"Would you go if you could?" Robby wasn't done.

In the car now, Jack felt trapped. Sally gave him a look that said she was curious how he would answer, and he knew Robby would insist that he give one. "I would think about it," he said grudgingly.

"Would you really, or are you just saying that?"

He had thought about it, and he didn't know why. He was still thinking about it even now. But he knew he couldn't go. What he and Sally had told Robby's friends was true. "I would really," he told his son.

That night Robby couldn't get to sleep. His mind skipped from one problem to another. He was concerned that his dad would go back to the way he was last winter because he didn't get that job. Then there was that business about his dad going on the mission. Ben and Chelsea had told everyone how much fun they had working at Alice's. Ben had really wanted Jack to go. And of course there was his constant companion. The clock was ticking; he was going to have to do it. He went to sleep still trying to figure out what to say.

CHAPTER 25

It was eight o'clock Monday morning, and Jack was the only one up. He had scrubbed through the want ads at breakfast like he did every day. And like every day, it was a waste of time. He knew Sally would start in on him again about calling Solar Systems. He just couldn't bring himself to do it. It would be more humiliation than he wanted to deal with.

Jack started going through his file of applications, looking for some it might be worth checking up on. He worried about calling too often and becoming a pest. But almost everyone was pleasant and told him to keep trying.

He was debating which call to make first when Megan crawled up on his lap. "You're a real sleepyhead," he said. "It's almost nine o'clock."

"Cassie and I have been awake. We were just talking."

Jack was pouring milk on Megan's cereal when he got the first phone call. The sound of the telephone roused the others, and by the time he hung up, they were all eating breakfast. "Well, at least I'm going to do that plumbing job," he announced without much enthusiasm.

"Today?" asked Sally.

"Tomorrow. Should get it done in a day." The kids parked in front of the TV, Sally went to get ready to go to work, and Jack started making phone calls. He talked to two companies and left his number at two others. He watched Sally get her lunch together and then walked her out to the car. "I really wish you would call that guy," she said.

"Sally, he was going to start second interviews today. He's already talking to the ones he wants."

"I think you should make him explain himself."

Jack went back inside and started to pick up the papers he had spread on the table. Then he got the second phone call. It was Solar Systems.

"We're really sorry about the short notice, but things have been crazy around here since Friday," the voice was saying. "We had a power outage Thursday night and are just getting back into production. John has been on the phone constantly trying to mollify customers. He would like you to come in after lunch if you can."

"What time?" Jack was trying to clear his mind. He wasn't really sure he knew what the woman had just said.

"Whenever you can get here."

"One o'clock?"

"John would appreciate that."

Jack went into the living room, where the kids were watching TV. He picked up the remote, waited for a commercial, and shut the TV off. Before they complain he held up his hand for silence. "I need two minutes," he said. "I just got a call from Solar Systems to come in for a second interview."

They all started talking at once. Jack waited them out and then told them what the woman had said. "This still doesn't mean that I have a job, but I'm one step closer," he explained. "I don't know how long this will take, so if it gets late you guys start dinner."

Jack was still dazed when he arrived at Solar Systems a few minutes before one, and more than a little nervous. John was waiting at the reception desk and ushered Jack right into his office. He told Jack about the chaos of the past few days and apologized for keeping him in suspense. "I was pretty sure I wanted to have you back for a second interview, but I had to follow the rules. You don't have any experience doing what we do here, but not very many people do. It's a very young industry. So what we are looking for are people who have the ability and willingness to learn new things. We also like for our people to be dependable and expect them to be responsible citizens. So far you get high marks in all cases."

Jack waited, not sure if he was expected to respond. "Thank you," he said after an uncomfortable silence.

"Okay." John stood up. "Let's take you for a walk through the plant."

Jack was amazed at how well lit, modern, and clean the plant was compared to the one he had worked in for twenty years. John walked him through all the various stations and departments, explaining the many operations and techniques they used. After a while, his mind refused to absorb any more information. *I hope I don't have to tell him what I remember*, he thought.

Back in the office, John asked him, "What did you think?"

Jack shook his head. "I think that was a whirlwind tour."

John laughed. "A lot to absorb. Do you have any questions?"

"I thought of one every ten steps while we were out there. I wouldn't know where to start."

"Did you see anything you thought you couldn't learn to do?"

"No, but some things were more interesting to me than others."

"We usually have our employees learn a little bit about each operation and then decide where they would be best suited."

John picked up a paper. "I called your references." He waved the page of notes at Jack. "They all had good things to say about you—without hedging. I can tell when people are just trying to say something good so they won't hurt someone's chances of being hired. They told me what I wanted to know without me asking a lot of questions. Because the power outage put me so far behind, I've been given some freedom to speed up the process. We'd like you to come to work for us."

Jack had been getting more encouraged as the interview went on, but this caught him completely by surprise. "Okay," he blurted.

"Okay." John smiled. "I'm going to turn you over to Trisha , and she will walk you through a mountain of paperwork."

John took Jack to another office and introduced him to Trisha. After John left, Trisha gave him a lot of forms to fill out that he didn't think existed when he started his first job. At least he didn't remember them. When he was finished and Trisha had checked everything over, she said, "I'm glad you got the job. I'm the one who overlooked your application. I feel really bad."

Jack was puzzled by her confession. "Did you get in trouble because of it?"

"Kind of. He wasn't very happy with me."

Jack couldn't think of anything else to say. He thanked her, they shook hands, and he left.

It was almost four o'clock when Jack got back to his truck. He sat there enjoying the giddy feeling. He couldn't believe this had happened. How it happened. His mind ran over the rollercoaster of emotions he had been through the past few weeks. It seemed like just yesterday that he thought about spraying Don with the hose when he came to his house to offer him a job. *I sure wouldn't be sitting here now*, he told himself. The whole thing was a blur.

His thoughts turned to his family. He wanted to go right over to Walmart and tell Sally to quit. He wanted to see the worry disappear from her face. He wanted to take his children on a vacation. He wanted to buy them things they didn't need. He started the truck and headed home.

When he pulled in the driveway, Robby, Cassie, and Megan came out to greet him. "Did you get dinner started?" he asked as he got out of the truck.

"We just got some stuff out, but that's all," said Cassie.

"Good. Put it away." He smiled. "I've got another job for you."

"What?" asked Cassie.

"I want you to get your heads together and come up with a nice restaurant that we can take your mother to for dinner."

Cassie broke into a smile. "What happened!"

"A job happened. They hired me." Cassie ran to him and threw her arms around him, with Megan close behind. "Will you stop worrying now?" He could feel her head go up and down against his chest.

"I will, Daddy," said Megan.

Jack looked over at Robby, who was trying to form words, but no sound would come out. "What about you?" Jack asked.

Robby shook his head and exhaled. "How ... ?"

"I don't know how it happened. But it did. They wanted me from the start," Jack said. "But you didn't answer my question."

"Yeah," Robby said without much enthusiasm. "Wow, that's a relief."

But there's something else that you won't tell me about, thought Jack. "You're sure?"

"Yeah, this is great." Robby was unconvincing.

Cassie finally let go of Jack. "Can we pick any place we want?" she asked, wiping the wetness from her face.

"As long as it's somewhere that we can sit down, order our food, and someone will bring it to us."

"Do we have to dress up?" asked Megan.

"Something you would wear to school would be fine."

"Or church?"

"Or church."

In the end they picked the Rib Shack, a small local restaurant that they knew Jack liked. "Robby said he didn't care where we went," said Megan, "so Cassie and I decided." *I've got to get to the bottom of this,* thought Jack.

Sally was startled to see her family sitting in the living room waiting for her. "We're going to the Rib Shack!" squealed Megan, unable to contain herself.

Even Robby was able to grin at Sally's reaction. "Did you call that guy?" she asked Jack.

"Nope."

"They called him," said Cassie.

"I start to work Monday."

Sally was unable to speak. "I did the same thing, Mom," said Robby, watching his mother trying to make her voice work.

"Oh, Jack" was all she was able to get out. They stood there, locked in a hug, not saying anything.

"Not this again," said Cassie. They just ignored her.

After the kids went to bed, Jack and Sally had some time alone. Jack filled her in on all of the little details that didn't come up through dinner. She too was puzzled by Trisha's confession. "She told me she was so upset that she took the whole pile home and went through them again in case she missed any others."

"She did it on her own time?"

"I doubt that John even knows about it." Sally fell silent, thinking about the man at the bank who didn't seem to care about anyone.

"Robby acted kind of strange when I told the kids." Jack changed the subject.

"How?"

"I don't know; I can't exactly describe it. It was almost like it was bad news."

"That doesn't make sense."

"I know, but something's wrong," said Jack. "I have to find out what it is. He's going to cut Alice's grass Thursday, maybe I can get him to talk when we take the lawnmower over."

In his room Robby was wrestling with his monster again. His first thought when Jack told them he had a job was that now everything was fixed and he was going to break it again. And he only had four days left. His dad would be gone all day tomorrow and maybe part of the next day. He was going to cut Alice's grass on Thursday. What did that all matter? There was no good time. He prayed himself to sleep.

CHAPTER 26

After lunch on Thursday, Jack and Robby loaded the lawnmower and Robby's bike into the truck and Jack drove him over to Alice's. "I wish you'd tell me what's bothering you." Jack got right to the point after several blocks of silence.

"I'm okay," said Robby, staring out the window on his side of the truck.

"You don't seem very happy for someone who's starting a new job and going on an adventure in two days." *I don't think my dad ever cared or even noticed whether I was happy or not,* thought Jack.

"Just a lot of stuff to think about. I'll figure it out."

"Is there a girl mixed around in this somewhere?"

Robby slumped in the seat. *That's all I need is a girl asking me questions about why I seem unhappy.* "No, Dad, there's no girl."

After a long silence, Jack tried again. "Well, something is bothering you. Maybe I could help you work it out if I knew what it was."

Robby didn't say anything. "You're not going to tell me, are you?"

They were almost there. Robby waited until they were in the driveway and said, "No." He got out of the car while it was still moving and started getting his bike out of the back.

Jack saw Alice coming out of her door and knew he'd lost his chance. *Maybe Sally should give it a try,* he thought. *I want to know what's going on before he goes on that trip.*

Robby wheeled his bike back to the garage and parked it. "I hear your vacation is over," said Alice. Sally had called Alice right away on Tuesday to tell her the good news and make a date for shopping.

"Finally." Jack grinned.

"I could hear the smile in Sally's voice when she called me. Congratulations."

Robby walked back up to the truck, forcing himself to put on a happy face. "What do you think about all this, young man?" Alice asked him.

"What a relief" was all he could manage.

They unloaded the mower, and Robby started to the back of the yard. "You really got that cleaned up nice," said Alice. "Does it run?"

Robby stopped and turned the mower around. He pulled on the starter rope. He pulled again, and it started. He let it run for a few seconds and then shut it off. "You did that just to show off," said Alice, getting a genuine smile out of Robby.

"My dad put in a new spark plug, showed me how to sharpen the blade, and I cleaned it all up."

"Well, it sounds better than that old thing the other boy used; let's see what kind of a job it does."

Robby said good-bye to Jack and headed back to mow. Jack and Alice talked for a few minutes; then Jack left. Robby started out being careful but soon found his thoughts distracting him. He kept going over what he was going to say, even reciting it out loud. His mind cleared just in time to prevent him from mowing right over the top of Alice's peonies. He tried to imagine explaining his way out of that.

He finished mowing, put the mower in the garage, and was starting to trim when Alice stuck her head out the door. "Come in here and get something to drink," she said and closed the door. It was a hot day, and Robby knew it was no use arguing with her.

He plopped down at the kitchen table, and Alice handed him a glass of lemonade. "You're all sweaty," she said. "How can someone as skinny as you sweat?"

Robby couldn't think of an answer. Alice poured herself some lemonade and sat down across the table from him. "You look like you lost your last friend. Are you sick?"

Why do people keep asking me that? I must look like Eeyore; probably sound like him too. "I've just got a lot on my mind."

"You nervous about the work mission?"

"No, that's not it."

"This would go a lot faster if you didn't make me keep guessing," Alice persisted.

His resistance gone, Robby wilted. He sat his glass down, wiped the condensation off the outside, and rubbed it on his sweaty face. Alice waited. "Do you know what Heifer is?"

Alice thought about that. "Is that the contraption with the tube that they collect the quarters in?" Robby nodded.

"They have that thing sitting so high I can't reach it, so I stopped saving my quarters. What about it?"

"You know someone took it last winter," said Robby.

"It was there last Sunday; I saw someone putting quarters it."

"Someone found it in that room behind the altar—empty."

Alice was getting a bad feeling. "I suppose you did it." Her face was unreadable.

Robby nodded again. "Why?" she asked.

Robby exhaled. "I thought that it would be enough money to help with expenses."

"How much was it?"

"Fifty-eight dollars and twenty-five cents."

"Hardly worth it." Robby nodded in agreement.

"When did you give it back?" Robby just looked at her. *How did she know?* "I figure anyone who was as worried about it as you are would give it back. Knowing you, I'm not surprised."

Robby told her the whole story. She listened without interrupting. "You gave that money back in February and haven't told your parents?" she asked after he had finished.

"Things were bad enough for them; I didn't want to add that to their problems. They didn't need to know their son was a thief."

"So now you're a thief." Robby rattled the ice cubes around in his empty glass. Alice got the pitcher from the counter and poured him some more lemonade.

"Have you ever told a lie?" she asked him. More silence. "Course you have. Here and there at least. Does that make you a liar?"

"That's not going to work. I took the money. It's not the same."

"It is the same, Robby; maybe not as bad. You gave the money back—no harm done. It's hard to repair the damage caused by a lie."

"My parents won't see it that way."

"How do you know? What did you think I was going to say? Or didn't you care?" Alice added with a smile.

"I felt safe telling you."

Alice wasn't expecting that. She waited until she was sure she could keep her voice steady. "Don and Jay both have pointed out the good things that have happened to you and your family because you took that money. Do you think that's all there is to it?"

"I don't know what you mean?"

"You don't think my life has been affected because you took that money?"

Robby felt ashamed. Of course it had affected her. It had been years since she had so much attention—people coming and going; his mother taking her shopping; his sisters spending hours with her. Big changes in her lonely life. "I'm glad it has, but what I did was still wrong."

"It was—no one will argue that——but everyone will forgive you; God has forgiven you. You need to forgive yourself. Get rid of the pain. Tell your parents."

Robby rode home slowly, thinking about his conversation with Alice. They had talked some more when he finished the trimming, and she paid him. "Maybe it won't be as bad telling your parents now that you've had me to practice on," she had joked. But he still felt only dread. Alice had convinced him that he should tell them tonight and not the night before he was leaving on the mission.

Robby paced the floor in his room, waiting for his mother to come home, hoping his sisters would go to bed before she did. He didn't want them to hear it. When he got home from Alice's, he had taken a shower and then "rested" until dinner. He cleaned up the kitchen after dinner and then busied himself in his room getting things together for the work mission. Jay had given them a list of things they would need.

He peeked out into the living room and saw that his sisters were still watching TV. Jack was reading a magazine. He hoped his mother had an easy day and wouldn't be so tired. He lay back down and went over his speech again. He heard his mother's voice and felt his heart start beating faster. It was almost ten o'clock. He heard his sisters put up a mild protest about going to bed, and then it got quiet. He whispered a short prayer and went out into the living room.

Jack was just coming from the kitchen with a glass of iced tea for Sally, who was lying back on the couch with her shoes kicked off. "Hi, Robby; they said you were asleep."

Robby felt numb all over and it was hard to breathe. "I need to talk to you." His voice was barely audible.

Sally sat up. "Are you all right?" Jack set Sally's tea on the end table and went over to Robby. Robby pulled away and sat down in a chair.

"I need to tell you something, and I don't want you to start yelling at me."

Jack and Sally looked at each other. "We won't yell," Jack assured him. *Finally he's going to talk*, he thought and sat down beside Sally.

"We'll just listen," said his mother.

Robby closed his eyes. *Please, God, help me do this*, he pleaded. He took a deep breath and started. "Do you remember last winter when Cassie brought that Heifer book home?"

They both nodded. "Do you remember what she said about why Don came to talk to them about Heifer at the after-school program?"

Jack knew he had been only half listening. Sally thought back, trying to remember. *What is this all about?* "Wait. Yes, it was because some… Oh, Robby." She covered her face with her hands. "Why…? I know why. Oh, Robby."

Jack broke his silence. "Do I get to know what this is all about, or do I start yelling?"

That eased the tension a little for Robby. "The reason Don talked to the after-school kids was because someone stole the Heifer peace pipe with all the quarters in it." Robby waited for his dad's reaction. He saw a look of understanding spread across his face. Then Jack stood up and let out a loud groan. Robby shrank back in his chair.

"That's what he meant," Jack said aloud to himself, pacing around the room, remembering his conversation with Don at the restaurant. "Don knows, doesn't he? And Jay too," Jack added before Robby could answer.

"Now we don't know what you're talking about," said Sally.

"Don told me that the reason good things were happening to us was because God hooked us up with the church and that I needed to understand that." Jack stopped pacing and looked at Robby. "Don thinks that's how God did it." Jack sat down.

"No, he doesn't," said Robby, his courage returning. "I did it because I was stupid. Don says God made me sorry for doing it, and that's why I called him. If I hadn't been sorry for doing it, nobody would have ever figured it out, and I would have never known Don."

Sally's head was spinning. Jack was more than curious. "What did you do with the money?"

"I gave it back." He told the story again like he had that afternoon, and they too listened without interruption. The prolonged silence when he was finished increased Robby's discomfort. "You're not mad?" he asked.

"Not yet," said Jack. "It hasn't sunk in yet." Jack was not happy with what Robby had done, but he would deal with that later. Right now his mind was in turmoil over what Don had said to him. If Robby had not taken that money, he would not have a job and their home would be in foreclosure with no hope of stopping it. So many things had changed in their lives because of it.

"Robby, why didn't you tell us right away?" asked Sally. "You carried that awful burden around for so long."

"I was ashamed. I didn't want you to be ashamed of me." Robby's resolve was weakening.

"I'm not ashamed of you, Robby. You made a mistake, and you corrected it. I'm proud of you for that. And I'm proud of you for caring for your family so much to do that." Robby was close to tears.

"Your mother's right," said Jack. "You put yourself at risk for your family. I would never have had the guts to do what you did when I was your age. It was wrong, but it was brave." That did it. Robby couldn't hold back the tears. All the long months of anguish poured out of him.

Sally went over and knelt beside him. She put her arms around him and cried with him. Jack walked behind his chair and put his hands on Robby's shoulders, gently kneading them to comfort him. The only sounds for a long time were occasional muffled sobs from Sally and Robby.

Sally released her hold on Robby and kissed him on the cheek. "Don't ever keep something bottled up inside you like that again," she said, sounding like she had a cold.

"Jay said you were made of tough stuff," said Jack. "He was right." Robby looked up at his dad and saw that he had tear stains on his face.

"I'm just so sorry."

"So am I, Robby," said Jack, sitting across from him now. "But I have to take some of the blame for this."

Robby shook his head. "I knew you'd say that."

"I say that because I wasn't handling the situation well, which caused more anxiety for all of you. If I would have had my head on straight, you wouldn't have been so worried and wouldn't have taken that money."

"But, Dad—"

"I know. None of the other things would have happened. I can't make sense of that. But I do know that lecture you gave me the day we got the foreclosure notice changed the way I looked at things."

"See, Robby, you can't think of yourself as a bad person. You're a good person," said Sally. "In the end you did the right thing. Give yourself credit."

Back in his bedroom, Robby was unable to get to sleep, something he had grown accustomed to. He thought that problem would go away when he finally told his parents about taking the money. Not tonight, though. He kept replaying the events of the day, astounded by the reactions to his story. He was much less anxious now about the next time he had to tell it. Jay wanted him to tell the mission team sometime during the week. "I think they should hear it right from you and not from all the hearsay that could go around," Jay had told him. But for now he had passed the hardest test and was greatly relieved. He fell asleep with a prayer of thanksgiving on his lips.

CHAPTER 27

Friday turned out to be a special day for Robby. Not only had he been relieved of a huge burden, but his dad got involved in preparations for the work mission. Jay called around ten o'clock to see if Jack would be willing to pick up the trailer they were going to take. The person he had lined up to do it had something unexpected come up and wouldn't be able to. Jack was away getting the insurance reinstated on his truck but came home a short time later.

"Sure, we can do that," Jack said with no hesitation. "When does he want it done?"

"Anytime this afternoon. He said to call, and he would give you the details."

After Jack had all the information he needed to pick up the trailer, Jay asked him, "Did you take that job just to get out of going with us?"

"How'd you guess?"

"Congratulations. It has to be a great relief."

"Thank you. It is."

"Anything else exciting going on over there?"

"You knew all about it, didn't you?" asked Jack

"I just told him it would be better for him to do it before the mission. He's been beating himself mercilessly for four months. Now he's done with it—almost."

"What do you mean?"

"He's going to tell his story to the mission team next week," Jay answered.

"He didn't tell us that."

"After what he's just gone through, it'll be easy for him."

"I hope so." Jack wasn't sure.

They went to get the trailer around three and parked it between the garage and the playground, where Jay wanted it. "Jay tells me you're going to tell the whole group about the quarters next week," said Jack on the way home.

"Yeah." Robby nodded.

"Are you sure you want to?"

"I don't want to wish I had later," said Robby. "Jay's going to make a program lesson out of it."

"How?"

"He says he can teach about all kinds of stuff from it. Bad choices, honesty, forgiveness, faith—a of lot stuff." Robby paused. "Trust."

Jack looked over at him. "I hope that's not a problem anymore."

"It's not."

Just as they turned into the driveway, Robby said, "Dad, there's something else I want to talk to you about."

"What is it?" asked Jack, shutting off the engine.

"I want to join the church."

"Why?"

"I've learned a lot of stuff that's starting to make sense to me about God and Jesus. Jay has taught me everything I need to know to become a member. The main thing is that you have to dedicate yourself to God.

I feel like I'm ready to do that. I want to do it." Robby watched his father's face for a reaction. There wasn't any.

"Jay and Don—the whole church—have helped me get through the trouble I got myself into. I've been praying a lot. When I pray for help, it gives me courage—like last night just before I came out to talk to you and Mom. I've been thinking about it for quite a while, but I couldn't do it with that other thing hanging over my head."

"They wouldn't let you?" Jack felt some old feelings rising.

"No," said Robby, shaking his head. "I didn't want to until I faced that problem. Jay said it was up to me."

"So you think praying works?"

Robby hesitated. "I've been praying for you to get a job for a long time. I know all those guys who helped you at Alice's are praying for you. Jay prays for things like that at the end of every youth group meeting." Robby could see his father's jaw tensing.

Jack didn't want to get into another discussion about how everything was happening because Robby gave the money back. He also didn't want to have a disagreement with his son the day before he left on his trip.

"Have you talked to the preacher?" *Does he know what Robby did?*

"Just once. He said to let him know when I was ready, but I have to be baptized."

"Are you asking for my permission?"

Robby hesitated again. "I'd rather have your support. I know you have bad feelings about the church."

Jack thought over his response to that. "I don't have bad feelings about this church. How could I?" Robby gave him just a hint of a smile. "What does that mean?" Jack asked.

"I was just thinking about what Alice said to you when I sprayed lemonade all over her kitchen."

"Do you think that's happening?" asked Jack. He remembered Alice's remark about the church sneaking up on him.

"I guess I want it to."

"Have you talked to your mother?"

"About joining the church? Yeah."

"No problem there, I'm sure," said Jack. Robby shook his head no. "Do we have to sign anything?"

"No, but you have to go to a meeting with me."

"What kind of meeting?" Jack was getting suspicious.

"Pastor Scot wants to make sure everyone understands exactly what I'm doing."

"Do you know exactly what you're doing?"

"Yes, I do. I know I do," said Robby, leaving no doubt. "But, Dad, there's so much more to it than I've just said. I know you had a bad experience when you were growing up, but I haven't. You had all those problems with your parents. I've never had any problems with my parents." Then Robby added with a crooked smile, "Except sometimes my dad can be a stubborn, hard guy."

"Like insulting your friends?"

"They're pretty hard to insult," said Robby. "I just wish you'd start all over and learn about it from this church."

Jack got out of the truck. "I'll talk to your mother. I don't see why you can't join the church if that's what you want." He started to say something else but stopped himself and went into the house.

Now what have I done? thought Robby, climbing out of the truck. He had not intended to throw a challenge at his dad and wondered if he had gone too far. He thought back over their conversation and ended up satisfied that Jack had taken what he said seriously.

That evening Jack sat with Sally while she ate a late dinner. "You're awfully quiet," she said. Jack just shrugged. "Still thinking about what Robby told us last night?"

"No, I'm thinking about what he told me this afternoon," he said.

"Now what?" Sally said uneasily.

"He wants to join the church. I guess you already knew about that."

"We've talked about it several times."

"Why didn't you say something?"

"He asked me not to. Robby wanted to talk to you himself without any influence from me," explained Sally. Jack thought about that.

"What did he say?"

"He said he's never had any problems with his parents like I had with mine." Jack paused.

"That's nice. Go on."

"Except sometimes his dad can be a stubborn, hard guy." Sally choked on a mouthful of food.

"And what did you say to that?" she asked, laughing. Jack folded his arms across his chest. "You didn't get mad, did you?" Sally was serious again.

Jack unfolded his arms. "No." He sighed. "He was grinning when he said it. He's learning way too much from those jokers at church."

And so are you. Sally smiled to herself. *Whether you want to or not.* "So you were a good sport about it?"

"I guess. I couldn't think of an argument. I just can't get his comment about my parents out of my mind." Sally waited, expecting more. "I should have some good memories, but I can't think of many. I can't remember being read to, playing games, going on vacation, going for ice cream, or any of the stuff we've done with our kids." Jack stopped again. Sally let him think it through. "Could I be so angry I won't let myself remember those things?"

Wow, could that be possible? Sally wondered. "Why don't you ask them if you ever did any of those things?" Sally knew she was on thin ice.

"I haven't seen or talked to them in five years." He scowled.

"What if one of them gets sick?" She felt the ice cracking. She had asked him that before.

"Don't start," said Jack, starting to clear away her empty dishes. Jack was in no mood to defend himself about that.

Sally decided to change the subject. "Did you give Robby an answer?"

"I told him that we would talk, but I could think of no reason not to if that was what he wanted to do. What have you been telling him?"

"I've been encouraging him."

"What about you?" he asked her.

"Joining the church?" Sally hesitated. "I won't do it alone."

"So you're going to blackmail me?"

"For a while at least."

Robby was awake before his alarm went off. The sun was streaming in his window, as promised by the weatherman. He got dressed and went quietly to the kitchen. His dad was already there.

"You're not excited, are you?" asked Jack.

"Not that much." Robby laughed. "Why are you up?"

"I've woken up early since Wednesday. I guess I'm excited too. There's a lot going on around here."

"Well, there's a lot going on in here," said Sally sleepily as she plopped into a chair. "Why are you up so early?"

"We're excited!" they said in unison. Sally wasn't amused

Jack wisely poured her a cup of coffee and sat it in front of her. Robby was already started on what would be his first bowl of cereal. He looked over at Jack. "Did you get a chance to talk to Mom?"

Jack raised his eyebrows, not expecting the question. "Yes, I did, and we agreed that you should do it." *That's interesting*, thought Sally. *Where was I when that happened?*

Robby and his parents arrived at the church just before seven o'clock. About half of the team was already there, and two more cars were coming right behind. Mike walked over to them. "Congratulations, Jack," he said, shaking his hand firmly. "You've got to be happy."

"Thank you. I am," said Jack.

"Jay stuck me with supervising the trailer loading; would you like to climb in there with me and help stack those bags so they all fit?"

"Be glad to," said Jack, and they walked over toward the trailer. *Yes!* thought Robby, doing a fist pump.

With Jack and Mike in the front of the trailer and two other parents in the back, the kids started bucket-brigading the bags in. They pushed the last bags in, and Mike closed the doors. Jay was starting to assemble everyone to the side of the playground when Jack noticed a woman striding purposefully toward him. "You must be Jack. I don't see anyone else I don't know," she said, holding out her hand. "I'm Karen. I team-teach these kids with Don."

Jack shook her hand. "I've heard good things about you from my family."

"That makes us even." Karen smiled. "Jay is just thrilled that Robby is going on this mission," she went on before Jack had a chance to respond.

"He's pretty excited."

She took his arm and steered him over toward where Jay was frantically trying to assemble the whole group into one big circle. "And I hear that you have a job? You must be excited."

"I am," he said. Sally and Robby waved to them across the circle, so they went over and joined them. They exchanged greetings quickly and then gave their attention to Jay. After giving them some last-minute instructions, he asked Pastor Scot to send them off with a prayer.

They joined hands around the entire circle. "Gracious God," Scot began, "we come to you on this beautiful morning to ask your blessing on our mission team. Keep them safe and well as they serve you by serving those who have suffered misfortune. Fill them with your spirit throughout the week so that people will know that they are disciples of Jesus. Keep them ever mindful that they may be the only glimpse of him that some people have ever seen. We pray that they will work hard, have fun, and bring back stories that will inspire the rest of us. We love you, we praise your name, and we thank you for all your goodness. All glory, honor, and praise to you. We pray these things in the name of Jesus. Amen."

Jack had never heard a prayer like that. Not that he ever paid much attention. There were no angry words, no threats, no begging for mercy, only requests for good things and thankfulness. Jack had been worrying that Robby would get sick or hurt or he wouldn't have fun like he expected. Scots words left him strangely comforted.

Robby gave them both hugs and got in one of the vans. Sally squeezed Jack's hand hard as the caravan left the parking lot and disappeared down the street. Their son had never been away from home for more than a day without them. Now he was going away for a week.

Jack had a lump in his throat, and he wondered whether he or Sally was going to start crying first.

CHAPTER 28

Robby was having the time of his life, but by Wednesday he was getting really anxious to know how his dad was doing. He mentioned it at lunch, and Ben said, "Call him and find out."

"We can't call home except for emergencies; you know that."

"Tell Jay you're so worried you're having trouble breathing," offered Ken.

"I think he should make an exception," said Jackie.

"We could go on a hunger strike if he won't," said Max.

"You go on a hunger strike," said Ben. "There are some things I don't give up."

"Maybe if we just explained it rationally to Jay he would see that it made sense," said Karla.

"Boring," said Max.

In the end they decided to tell Jay that they all thought it was a reasonable request and that he should allow it. When they told him at dinner, he said he agreed and Robby could call in between dinner and the evening program. "That was way too easy," said Max later.

Excited and nervous, Robby dialed Jay's cell phone. He had let himself worry that Solar Systems had changed their mind or that his dad didn't like the job. Everybody was assembled in the room, enjoying the moment. Jack answered the phone. "Hi, Dad."

Before Jack could say anything he heard a loud chorus of "Hi, Dad's" from the whole group. "What's going on?"

"Everyone wants to know how your job's going, so Jay let me use his phone to call."

"It's going great. It's really interesting, and I like all the people I'm working with."

"Really?" Robby gave the room a thumbs up.

"Really. How are you doing?"

"I can't believe it's Wednesday already. It seems like we just got here." People were starting to drift away or get involved in their own activities. Robby moved over to the side of the room.

"What are you doing?"

"We're rebuilding a handicapped ramp that got wrecked in the flood for a woman who's about as old as Alice. But she's not anything like Alice."

"Nobody's anything like Alice." Jack laughed.

"I'm glad you like your job."

"Were you worried?"

"Kind of."

"You don't need to be. Enjoy the rest of your week. I'm proud of you for doing this, Robby. I can't wait to hear all about it."

"Thanks, Dad. Give everyone a hug for me. I miss you all."

During the sharing time that night, Karla and Ken confessed that their crew felt like they were wasting their time on the job they had been assigned to that day. The work project's supervisor, Chuck, had asked Jay to send a crew to knock down the weeds in an overgrown field, so Jason sent another adult, Derek, along with Karla, Ken, and Troy to take care of it.

"All we're doing is using weed whackers to mow a great big field," said Ken. "It's completely surrounded by overgrown hedges that they want us to start trimming tomorrow."

"There's an opening in the hedges to get into the area from behind this little house," added Karla. "But it doesn't even look like anyone lives there."

"It's pretty frustrating after working on that drywall job for two days and getting to know the family we're working for," said Troy. "Those little kids are fun."

"What do you think, Derek," asked Jay.

"Well, I wasn't thrilled with the job either, so after dinner I went over and talked to Chuck. He told me that the old man who lives there is sort of an icon around here. He grows seedlings of all kinds of trees and bushes in his basement over the winter, plants them in the spring, and then gives them away to people all over the area in the fall. He had a stroke this winter right after he planted the seeds, and then the flood came. They were able to rescue the seedlings, but the high water made it impossible for them to be planted. He even had volunteers lined up to plant them for him, but of course they couldn't. Chuck has been looking for a chance to get someone in there to knock down the weeds enough to rototill the field. The old man thinks the seedlings might still grow enough to survive the winter and he can give them away next spring. We're the first group with enough people for Chuck to get started on it. He said the old guy is pretty depressed anyway, and his wife thinks it might cheer him up."

"I feel better already," said Ken.

"We've got two more days. Maybe we can finish it," said Karla.

"Maybe we could start on the rototilling," added Troy.

"You guys are awesome," said Jay proudly.

By late morning the next day, Ken and Troy were almost finished knocking down the weeds. Karla and Derek had the hedges across the back trimmed and were starting down one side when they noticed a woman watching them from the opening by the house. Karla and Derek put down their hedge clippers and signaled for Troy and Ken to do the same. She made no move toward them, so they went over to her.

"Hello, can we help you?" asked Derek.

The woman was sad and worn-out looking and seemed extremely nervous. "My name is Cheryl," she started and then hesitated. "My parents live here." She motioned back over her shoulder.

They all introduced themselves and shook hands with her. "You people are so kind. My parents are so grateful for what you are doing." Cheryl was struggling with her emotions. "This has been very hard on them."

"And you too, I'll bet," said Derek.

"My mother is in a wheelchair. My dad was able to take care of her until he had his stroke. Now it's just me."

"We're having fun doing this," said Ken. "Can we meet them?"

"That's why I'm here," said Cheryl, seeming to relax a little. "They want you to come in for lunch."

"In their house?" said Troy. "We're all grungy."

"Their house is used to grungy." Cheryl almost smiled. "With my dad traipsing in and out with plants all the time," she added.

They cleaned themselves up the best they could and then followed Cheryl inside. She introduced them to her parents. Sophie was hunched down in her wheelchair, small and fragile looking with snow white hair. Otto was sitting in a recliner, the effects of the stroke obvious on the right side of his body.

"You kids are going to save all my little plants for me," he said slowly, trying to force his face to smile. "I've been praying that Chuck could find someone who was willing to do it. It's a long, hard job in this hot weather, and I can't thank you enough." They waited patiently while he labored to get the words out.

"We weren't happy about doing it until we found out what you used it for," said Troy honestly.

"Now we're glad for the chance," said Karla. "We'd like to get far enough to plant some trees." Otto couldn't stop smiling.

"We've been giving those trees and bushes away for twenty years," said Sophie, her voice clear and strong, not at all like her frail body. "Some to people as far away as fifty miles."

They enjoyed a lunch of shredded beef sandwiches, fresh carrots, potato salad, and lemonade. Sophie told them that Cheryl had spent the morning preparing the food. More than the food, they enjoyed listening to Otto's endless string of stories sprinkled with frequent corrections of dates and names from Sophie. It was almost two o'clock when Derek finally suggested that they go back to work.

"You should take them to the basement and show them the plants," Otto said to Cheryl in his raspy voice that had faded to almost a whisper.

"I wanted to ask if we could," said Ken.

Cheryl led them down to the basement. There were three feet-deep tables built around the entire perimeter of the basement. Every square inch of surface was covered with plantings, all carefully identified.

"We need to get at least a small area ready big enough for everyone in the group to plant at least one tree," said Troy.

Back outside, they worked with renewed energy. By consensus they decided to work an hour past their usual quitting time of four o'clock. They went back to the church where they were staying tired and hungry but eager to tell their story.

Their tone during share time that night was far different than it was the night before. They excitedly told about their plan to have the whole group plant some trees. Jay said that all the other crews could quit at three o'clock the next day so they could plant a tree and meet Sophie and Otto.

"I think you all have to admit that we have the best story of the week," bragged Ken.

You are going to eat those words, bubba, thought Jay, glancing over at Robby, who was sitting with his head down.

Later, in bed, Robby was having serious second thoughts. He felt his courage to tell his story again rapidly slipping away. The magical week had kept his mind off of it, but now it was staring him in the face again. His old fears of being condemned as a thief had returned. He dreaded what he would hear from his friends. Would he even have friends anymore? He once again turned to God and prayed himself to sleep.

On Friday Chuck delivered two rototillers to Sophie and Otto's. Ken and Troy started in the back corners of the area, while Derek and Karla finished trimming the hedges. Just after three the others started arriving. Troy and Ken wheeled Sophie out to the nursery area, while Ben and Robby walked Otto out. When Otto first saw his almost restored nursery, he was overcome. His legs buckled, and Ben and Robby had to hold him up until Jackie brought a chair for him to sit on. Through his tears he finally garbled out, "It's beautiful."

Karla lined everyone up to take their turn going to the basement to pick out a tree or bush.

After they had all made their choices, they made a big circle around Sophie, Otto, and Cheryl, who had just arrived. Jay offered a prayer of dedication.

"Holy God, we thank you for the opportunity to help restore Sophie and Otto's nursery. The blessing is ours. As we place these trees and bushes in the ground, may we be reminded that it is you, not us, who will make them grow. We pray that you will continue to heal Otto so he may once again be able give to others as he has for so many years. We pray, as always, in your Son's name. Amen."

Otto instructed them how to properly plant the seedlings. When they were done, he told them that he would not give away what they had planted for three years as a memory of what they had all done for him.

He and Sophie thanked them again and again for all their hard work. They helped their new friends back into their home, said their sad good-byes, and left knowing that God was pleased with their efforts.

After the sharing time, Jay briefly reviewed the nightly programs. "We've talked about accepting the consequences for our decisions, passing judgment, forgiveness, courage, faith, and trust. Tonight I'm going to try to wrap all those things together, and I'm going to do it by having you listen to the testimony of maybe the bravest person I've ever known. I want you to listen quietly and not make any comments until he is finished. Then we will discuss his story."

Jay let that sink in for a few moments, watching them all glance around trying to figure out who he was talking about. He had talked to Robby just before the meeting and wasn't sure he would go through with it. He looked at him now and thought he saw a look of resolve. *Here goes*, he thought.

They were arranged in a haphazard circle, some sitting in chairs, some sitting on the floor, some lying on the floor on their pillows. Robby had chosen to sit on a chair in a space where he wasn't right next to anyone.

"Okay," said Jay. "I want you all to give your attention to Robby."

Robby felt everyone's eyes on him and didn't think he was going to be able to speak. He looked at Jay and got a smile of encouragement. His voice cracked when he started, but he was able to calm down and talk normally. He told the story from the beginning and spared them no details. He told them about his remorse, his agony, his fear of isolation, his feeling that he had betrayed his family, the courage and comfort he got from praying, and his great relief when he finally told his parents.

When he was finished the room stayed quiet. Jay let the silence linger for a few minutes.

"Was I right that all the things we've talked about this week are in Robby's story? I'm going to let you guys ask the questions. Anybody got one?" No one spoke. Jay waited.

"What is there to ask?" Ben broke the silence. "He answered every question you could think of in his story." Ben was sitting the nearest to Robby, about a six-foot space between them. He moved his chair closer to Robby while he talked.

"He made a mistake. He corrected it. He suffered for it. He's still my friend." Ben looked at Robby and extended his fist toward him. They bumped fists. It was all Robby could do to keep from crying.

Chelsea, who was crying, spoke up. "Robby, I just feel so bad for you. You always seem so happy, but you were keeping that all inside. I know you explained why you waited, but I wish you would have told sooner."

Others began to chime in with their comments, all acknowledging the mistake, but all clearly passing no judgment. "I just can't believe you had the guts to do it," said Max. "I could never be that brave— even for my family. And then to admit it and give it back. You're my hero, dude."

Until that point none of the advisors had spoken. "I agree with everything that has been said, and for Robby's sake, those words need to come from his peers," said Julie. "I can't add anything to what you all have said. What I can say is how satisfying it is to watch and listen to the mature, understanding, and compassionate way you all have dealt with this. A perfect example of Christian love." All of the other advisors were nodding in vigorous agreement.

The room went silent again. "We haven't heard from Troy and Karla," said Jay. "Are we going to?"

"I think," Troy started and then stopped. "How should I say this? This is a great story, but here's how I see it. We've all been talking about how this all turned out for the good because Robby felt guilty and gave the money back. I think that's only the first step; anyone could do that. Give the money back, go on your way, and nobody's the wiser. But Robby didn't stop there. He turned it over to God, and then things started getting fixed. If he doesn't take the second step, there is no story."

"You guys don't need me." Jay smiled. "I'm learning stuff from you." He turned to Karla. "You have been strangely silent. Do you have any wisdom for us? No pressure."

Karla laughed. "I'm like Julie; I can't think of anything profound to add, but I think Troy really nailed it. Robby's story and all this discussion has given us all a lot to think about for a long time." Karla paused and then continued with an impish smile on her face. "We haven't known Robby very long, but we all love and respect him, and I think it's awesome how he has cleverly stolen his way into our hearts."

The adults got it right away and started laughing. Then the groans and boos started and wadded-up candy wrappers and junk food bags were flying in her direction. Karla sat there grinning through it all, very much enjoying her own humor.

Jay realized that the meeting was over, so he quickly repeated instructions for their early departure in the morning and dismissed them with prayer.

Jack and Sally waited nervously in the church parking lot with the rest of the parents. They had been called around one with the message that the mission team was about three hours away, so they went over at four. It was now almost five. None of the other parents seemed worried. Joanie told them that this wasn't unusual. "When you're traveling with eighteen teenagers, you can't predict how many pit stops you might have to make. Early estimates are not always accurate," she had said.

Jack's new job had distracted him from worrying about Robby, but Sally had been anxious all week. She felt cheated because she was at work when he called on Wednesday. She had no idea she would miss him so much. The girls had confessed that they missed him too. She watched them in an animated conversation with some other younger siblings who were also waiting. Sally was thinking about the changes in their lives since they started coming to this church when she heard someone shout, "Ten minutes! They're just getting off the expressway."

They lined up on both sides of the driveway where it emptied into the parking lot. Cassie and Megan stood with their parents, getting caught up in the excitement. Finally a shout went up, "There they are!" as the first van came into sight and turned into the driveway, followed closely by the other two, all honking their horns. Sally felt her eyes misting as she breathed a prayer of thanks.

Derek made the announcement that they were about fifty miles from home, but it was heard by fewer than half the passengers in the van. Some were sleeping and some were plugged into their iPods, while the rest were either playing on a DS or just talking. Robby was hooked up to his iPod but had it turned off. He was anxious to be home, but mostly he was excited about talking to Pastor Scot about joining the church. The past week had confirmed beyond a doubt that he wanted to give his life to Jesus. Troy's comment that all of these events had unfolded because Robby had turned to God had wiped away any doubts. But why had he turned to God? "Because he kept getting in your way," Jay had said to him. "Once you stopped trying to go around him, things started getting better."

Robby wondered if that was happening to his dad. His anger at the church seemed to be almost gone. Certainly he was in harmony with the people of this church. Was he still harboring anger toward his parents? Would his dad stand with him in the front of the church when he was baptized and confirmed? *Will I be able to accept it if he doesn't?*

It was going to happen in a week, when the work mission team gave its report to the congregation. Robby and Jay had talked about it several times during the past week. Jay had checked with Pastor Scot and cleared the way for it to happen. He did, however, insist on a meeting with Robby and his parents early in the week. Just as Robby started to worry about that he felt the van slow down as Derek turned onto the exit ramp. *Ten more minutes*, Robby said to himself as he joined the others in collecting all their belongings.

Robby's heart did a little thump when he saw his family standing there to greet them with the others. They could hear the cheers and applause as the vans, horns blaring, passed slowly between the two lines. Cassie and Megan were jumping up and down and clapping their hands. Robby climbed out and looked for his family. Before he could take two steps Cassie and Megan had him in a group hug. "Did you have fun?" "Are you glad to be home?" "Did you miss us?" They didn't give him a chance to answer their string of questions. Then his parents were there. He set his backpack on the pavement and gave his mother a long hug.

"I love you," Sally said through her tears and gave him a kiss.

"I love you, too, Mom." Robby was close to tears himself.

Robby thought Jack was going to squeeze all the air out of him. "Welcome back, son" was all he could manage to say.

Robby made the rounds saying good-bye to all his friends while Jack helped unload the trailer and put Robby's things in their van. All of the advisors made it a point to tell either Sally or Jack how much Robby had contributed to the success of the week. Mike just shook Jack's hand and said, "He's a keeper."

"Let's go get something to eat and start listening to stories," said Jack as they drove out of the parking lot. "Are you hungry?" he asked Robby.

"I need pizza," he answered.

CHAPTER 29

Robby was exhausted. The long trip, the emotional reunion with his family, and the endless storytelling had worn him out. But he had one more thing to deal with. He had to tell his sisters. His parents had agreed that they should hear it from him. It was a beautiful, warm summer evening, so the girls thought nothing of it when Sally told Jack that he was going for a walk with her.

"I can't wait till I'm old enough to go on a mission trip," said Cassie said to Robby for the third time.

"When you go on your first mission trip, I'll be going on my last one."

"I'll never be old enough," Megan pouted.

"I have to tell you guys something," said Robby. "I don't want to, but I don't want you to hear it from someone else."

"Hear what?" asked Cassie.

He told them a shorter story, leaving out the details of his many conversations with Don and Jay. "Does Alice know?" asked Megan when he was finished.

"Yes."

"What did she say?" asked Cassie.

"The same things everybody else says. It was wrong, but I made it right and I should quit worrying about it."

"Have you?" Cassie wanted to know.

Robby shook his head. "Not completely."

"If you didn't take those quarters Alice wouldn't be our friend," said Megan. Robby and Cassie just looked at each other. "And she would still be lonely and sad." More silence. "And Mommy wouldn't be happy because she gets to take Alice shopping."

"Alice said some things like that to me," said Robby.

"I'm glad you did it," Megan decided. "Alice is more important than that old money."

"I'm glad you gave it back, because that's what made all those things start to happen," said Cassie.

On Monday, Robby spent most of the morning cutting Alice's lawn. The lawn didn't take long, but the conversation afterward did. She wanted to know all about the work mission. She particularly liked the Otto and Sophie story. Robby asked her if she would come to the first worship service on Sunday and sit with his family.

"I'd be honored to do that." Alice seemed hesitant. "I'm trying to think who I know that goes to that service." Robby realized that she would need a ride.

"We'll pick you up," he said. "The whole family should go together," he added with a smile.

"I'll be ready."

After lunch Robby decided to go talk to Pastor Scot. Robby had talked to his parents on Sunday, and they said they could meet with him on Tuesday or Wednesday evening. He wasn't sure what Pastor Scot would say, so he didn't know what to expect out of his father. But it made him nervous. He was also anxious about what Pastor Scot would say about him taking the quarters. Jay had told him on Sunday that Pastor Scot wanted to talk to him about it.

He rode his bike through the parking lot and saw that the little red car wasn't there. But Jay's truck was. He went inside and found Jay in his office.

"Pastor Scot had a lunch meeting," said Jay. "He could show up anytime now. You can just hang out here and wait if you want to."

When a half hour had passed, Robby decided he shouldn't take any more of Jay's time. He was heading down the ramp on his bike when Pastor Scot drove in. Robby turned his bike around and rode over to where Pastor Scot had parked.

"Hi, Robby," he said. "Are you looking for me?"

"Jay said you wanted to talk to me." He seemed friendly enough, but Robby was still nervous.

Pastor Scot pointed in the direction of the playground. "How about over there at the picnic table in the shade?"

They sat across from each other, and Robby waited for him to start. "On a scale of one to ten, how do you rate the work mission?"

Robby had not expected that question. Feeling more comfortable he said, "Twelve."

Pastor Scot laughed. "I'm glad you feel that way. So you didn't come home with any scars?"

"No."

"I understand you had some scars healed."

Here we go, thought Robby. "One great big scar," he said.

After a pause, Pastor Scot said, "Do you know the story about the Apostle Peter on the night Jesus was arrested?"

"I'm not sure."

"Earlier in the evening Jesus had told Peter that he would deny that he knew him three times that night. Peter very confidently told

Jesus that he would do no such thing, but when things started falling apart and Jesus was put on trial, all the apostles became confused and frightened and ran away. Peter hung around to see what was happening to Jesus and three times was identified by someone as one of Jesus's followers. All three times Peter said they were mistaken, that he didn't know Jesus, something he regretted the rest of his life, even though Jesus clearly forgave him later." After a pause Pastor Scot added, "Do you see how that story applies to yours?"

"Sort of," said Robby.

"When we are desperate and frightened we sometimes do things that we would never do otherwise. I believe that if you hadn't been worried about what was happening to your family, taking those quarters would have never crossed your mind. I can't give you any better advice or any better support than you've already been given by Jay and your peers. You are a brave and honorable young man, and I am certain that God is pleased with you."

Robby didn't think that he could speak. "Thanks" he managed to mutter.

Pastor Scot changed the subject. "Do we have a time when I can meet with you and your parents?"

"Tuesday or Wednesday."

"I think Wednesday will work best for me," he said after some thought. "What does your dad think about all this?"

Robby told him what Alice had said to his dad about God sneaking up on him. "I think that's what's happening, and I think he knows it. I'm not sure about his problem with his parents, though."

"One thing at a time. Let's see if we can get him coming to church first."

That night in his room Robby thought over the things that Pastor Scot had said to him. He had at least expected a scolding, if not a lecture. But it was nothing like that. His friend Bob was the same way on Sunday morning. "You tortured yourself all those months for nothing. Next time, just ask; we'll take care of you," he had said after giving Robby his usual bear hug. Everyone who had found out what he had done clearly thought that it was wrong, but not one person had condemned him. Jay had told him it was grace, but Robby wasn't sure he understood what that was all about.

Robby and his parents arrived at the church just before seven on Wednesday. It seemed to Robby that there was some kind of meeting in every room. He could hear the sound of the choir practicing coming from the sanctuary. Pastor Scot came through the narthex from his office and led them to a small conference room that was furnished with a sofa and soft chairs. Scot offered Jack and Sally the sofa, and he sat across from them. Robby moved quickly to the recliner and made himself comfortable.

After a brief exchange of small talk, Scot directed his remarks to Jack and Sally. "I want to make sure you know how much this church cares for your family. People are really excited about what Robby is doing. I know your experiences with the church when you were young did not lead you in that direction, but we are hoping that, with God's help, we eventually can." Scot paused. "And I think we are already seeing some encouraging signs," he added with a smile, getting a smile back from Sally and a grin from Robby. Jack's face was unreadable.

Scot decided to let that sit. "Here's how Sunday will work: I will call you up to the front—you may have anyone you want stand with you—and we will do the baptism first and then move right to the membership ritual. Here are the questions you will be asked." He handed Robby two sheets of paper.

Scot went over each question with Robby, making sure he understood what he was promising to do. Jack listened with reluctant interest. Much of it was familiar, but the tone of it was far different than he had heard it before. Or was it, and he had just closed his mind to it then? *Would I have seen it differently if I had heard it this way, from this kind of preacher? Robby is so confident and comfortable with all of it.*

"Well, Robby, it looks like Jay has taught you well," said Scot. "I expected more questions. Do you have any?" He turned to Jack and Sally.

"All we do is stand up there?" said Sally.

"With Robby. You will be his main support group. He will need that to keep all of the promises he is making."

"I've asked Alice to come. Can she stand up there with us?" asked Robby.

"I think that would be the most important thing that has happened to her in many years." Scot smiled. "You all have put new meaning in her life. You are the family she never had."

When the silence started to get uncomfortable, Scot asked Jack, "Are you all right with all of this?"

Jack wanted to just say yes and leave; he did not want to get drawn into a discussion that would require him to defend himself. "This is very important to Robby, and I won't spoil it for him. He's old enough and mature enough to make these kinds of decisions for himself. Except for the obvious, he has always made good decisions. He has chosen well who to get advice from."

"So you support his decision to do this?"

"For him, yes."

"Fair enough, for now," said Scot.

"What does that mean?" Jack bristled. Robby squirmed in the recliner.

Scot thought for a minute. "Jack, I think I have a pretty good idea about all of your issues with the church and God, and given your experiences, I don't really blame you. But you have to understand that God never takes delight in the suffering of his children. Just like you never would yours. The trouble your family has just suffered through was unfortunate, but I think the prayers of a lot of people helped you through it. I know one of the things that really made you angry was the church offering you money—what you call charity. Our church family helps people financially when we can. When we help people it is not to make them feel less about themselves but to let them know that God loves them. We have helped a lot of people get back on their feet and then, when times are better, they help someone else in a similar situation. You know, that old 'pay it forward' movie idea. After you get comfortable with your new job and your life is more settled, you might reflect back over all this and see if you are looking at things through different eyes—your parents included."

Jack could feel Robby and Sally's discomfort. He didn't know what to say. "I haven't met anyone from this church I didn't like," he started. "I tried, but it didn't work. Everyone has been helpful and friendly in spite of my behavior. Through no fault of my own I might even have made some friends. But I have this unexplainable reaction when I get pressured about . . . church stuff. I guess I'll have to learn how to handle it better, but right now I can't."

Pressure is not good, thought Scot. *We need to be careful here.* "Perhaps we all should be more patient," he said, after some consideration. "You have my standing offer to talk about any or all of it whenever you want to."

When they got home, Jack went for a walk by himself. What Scot had said to him had unsettled him. Every time he tried to see things like his family did, flashbacks of his childhood resurfaced. He couldn't shake the feeling that he had somehow misjudged his parents; that things weren't as bad as he remembered them. But the memories were so vivid. Was he only remembering what he wanted to remember? The more he thought about it, the more confused he got.

CHAPTER 30

Robby woke up early. Finally it was Sunday! He lay in his bed and went over the list of questions Pastor Scot was going to ask him one more time. Since he had decided to declare his life for Jesus he had never wavered, and now he was excited to declare it publicly.

They left a little early to go pick up Alice. She was out of the door before the car stopped in the driveway. After they exchanged good mornings, Robby said, "Alice, I want you to stand up in front with us."

"No need for that."

Before Robby could say anything Jack spoke up. "Alice, this is a big day for Robby, and it matters a lot to him that all the important people in his life are up there to support him."

For once Alice had nothing to say.

There were two young people greeting churchgoers at the edge of the parking lot. Just inside the door Jack found himself being greeted by two more. Jack remembered that Robby had told him that the mission team was doing the worship service. A few steps later there was Mike. Then Bob saw him and came over to shake hands. At the entrance to the narthex, Cassie steered him over to two more greeters. "I didn't know I would have to run the gauntlet," he whispered to Sally.

"Get used to it," she whispered back.

They sat down nearer the front than usual so Alice wouldn't have so far to walk for the ceremonies. Jack was uncomfortable. He felt as though everyone was staring at him. It seemed as though he was moving in slow motion down the long aisle. When they got into their seats, he realized he was sweating.

Ken got up, welcomed everyone to the service, and then invited them to greet each other. Everyone was on their feet, shaking hands and hugging. Jack's mind was spinning from Sally introducing him and people introducing themselves. He felt a tug on his sleeve, and there was Scot reaching his hand past two people. Joe and Ed waved to him from across the church. *If this is a church, I've never been in one before,* he thought to himself. Sally, noticing the look on his face, leaned over to him and said quietly, "Get used to it."

Next they sang a hymn. Jack couldn't remember happy, smiling singing in his parents' church. Then Chelsea and Nikki called the grade-schoolers up for the children's sermon. Jack watched Megan jump up, squeeze her way out of the pew, and march to the front like she owned the place. Every time Chelsea or Nikki would ask a question, Megan's hand would be in the air and she spoke right up when she was called on. *What happened to my shy little girl?* Jack wondered.

The next part of the service was devoted to prayer. Ben and Troy took microphones around to anyone who wanted to ask for prayers for someone with special needs. People asked for prayers for everything from newborn babies to people still looking for work to the death of loved ones. *Did someone do that for me, and I didn't know it?* Jack asked himself.

Then Pastor Scot asked Robby and his family to come forward. Robby could hear his heart thumping. He hadn't expected to be nervous. Jack and Sally followed him to the altar area. Cassie and Megan walked up beside Alice and helped her up the steps. Jack looked out at the congregation, feeling very much out of place. He shifted his weight from one foot to the other and tried to figure out what to do with his hands through the entire baptism. It was all very strange to him. After he baptized Robby, Pastor Scot asked his family to lay their hands on him for a prayer, which made Jack feel all the more awkward.

Robby, on the other hand, felt as though he was floating on air. He answered all the questions with conviction and confidence. Although he knew he had been forgiven and had not been judged by anyone there, he experienced a great feeling of relief when Pastor Scot placed the water on his head. All the badness had been washed away. When his family put their hands on him as he knelt for the prayer, he knew exactly who each hand belonged to.

Before he started the ritual for joining the church, Pastor Scot invited anyone who would like to come up and stand with Robby to do so. Like a flock of birds, all of Robby's friends in the youth program instantly swept out of their seats and formed a circle around Robby and his family. Already emotionally charged, it was all he could do to keep from crying.

Jack was stunned and relieved. The whole thing was surreal, but the actions of the young people made him feel less conspicuous. He was moved, however, by the show of support from Robby's friends. *Did things like this happen at my parents' church and I missed it?*

After Robby had answered the questions for membership, Pastor Scot declared that he was now officially a member, and the congregation stood and applauded him. Jack was more astonished than ever. And confused. Surely his parents' church baptized people and took in new members. He had absolutely no recollection of it. What else had he blocked from his mind?

Several of the mission team members gave short talks on their experiences in Wisconsin. Jack felt a twinge of regret that he had been unable to go. He knew he would have if he had still been out of a job. He would have really enjoyed working with his son. All of the speakers said that the most meaningful part of the trip was the evening programs, especially the last night. None of them mentioned Robby's name.

After the service Jack went through another flurry of introductions and congratulations. He was able to separate himself from the crowd and watched his son exchange laughter and hugs with his friends. A smiling woman walked up to him.

"Hi, Jack. I'm Carol. Bob's wife."

"Hello, Carol." He shook her hand.

"I noticed the proud father watching his son interact with his friends."

Jack nodded. He was proud of his son.

"I can tell there's a lot of stuff whirling around up there," Carol said, obviously referring to Jack's head. *If she only knew*, thought Jack. *Or does she?*

"You'll get it sorted out. Most of us do sooner or later." Carol smiled. She patted him on the arm as she walked away, leaving him with his thoughts.

Alice walked up to him and said, "Got snuck up on, didn't you? Don't say I didn't warn you." And she walked away.

Robby had been looking for a chance to talk to Don but couldn't break away long enough to find him. He saw him walking toward the coffee bar and intercepted him. Don shook his hand and gave him a hug. "Thanks for listening to me all those weeks," said Robby.

"Thank you for putting up with me. You're not he same young man who called me back in February. You know where you're going now. It's my great privilege to be your friend, Robby braveheart." They embraced again.

Jack watched that exchange with a lump in his throat. He didn't know what words were spoken, but he knew that two friends had expressed their love for each other. Once again he thought about things he had missed.

Jack started collecting his family to leave. *We haven't had a vacation in over a year*, he thought. But he had no vacation time coming. The long Fourth of July weekend was coming up. Illinois was not that far. *Why not? Time to start over.* He'd tell his family on the way home.

AFTERWORD

The idea for this story came to me because of the incident that happens at the beginning of the book. In January of 2009, quarters were actually taken from the Heifer peace pipe at my church and the peace pipe was found hidden in the sacristy behind the sanctuary. There was a snowstorm that week, cancelling schools and the after-school program. The peace pipe was found in exactly the way I described. Everything beyond that point, except for the Heifer stories, is fiction; we simply have no clues.

Many of the characters, however, are real people being themselves. I have tried to capture the rich flavor of the people in our church and have mostly used their real names in order to positively identify the guilty. Some characters are composites of people. Jeff, the helpful, friendly young man at the bank is real and helped me with all the loan/foreclosure rules. Robby and his family probably exist all over our country.

A special thanks to my friend Scot Ocke for his interest and support. He gave me some great ideas, and one of his speeches is actually his own words.

And, of course, I must thank Beverly, who once again graciously endured my long absences at the computer when her needs are much greater than mine.